TREE
DREAMS

TREE DREAMS

A NOVEL

KRISTIN KAYE

SparkPress, a BookSparks imprint
A Division of SparkPoint Studio, LLC

Published by SparkPress, a BookSparks imprint,
A division of SparkPoint Studio, LLC
Tempe, Arizona, USA, 85281
www.gosparkpress.com

Published 2018

Printed in Canada

ISBN: 978-1-943006-46-5 (pbk)
ISBN: 978-1-943006-47-2 (e-bk)
Library of Congress Control Number: 2017956949

Cover design © Julie Metz, Ltd./metzdesign.com
Formatting by Katherine Lloyd/theDESKonline.com

Printed on FSC-Certified paper

For Siddha, who will one day touch the sky
For Jem, who gives me roots
And for the redwoods that taught me.

To be whole. To be complete. Wildness reminds us what it means to be human, what we are connected to rather than what we are separate from.

—Terry Tempest Williams

… perhaps one day the language of trees will eventually be deciphered, giving us the raw material for further amazing stories. Until then, when you take your next walk in the forest, give free rein to your imagination—in many cases, what you imagine is not so far removed from reality, after all!

—Peter Wohlleben, *The Hidden Life of Trees:*
What They Feel, How They Communicate—
Discoveries from a Secret World

The old dream begins again: I stand in a forest under an inky dark sky. An oak tree looms before me with thick, snaking branches that kink and bend and grow, steady and slow, right before my eyes. Light shines from the tiny tips of each branch, the whole tree a glowing silhouette in the darkness. I have one single job: to name the light. I don't know how I know that I am meant to name the light or what will happen when I do—the trees and the light and I will become one, maybe. Or the tips will finally grow onto the ends of the branches and the tree can go back to being a tree. Or it could be that everything will stop growing out of control. How I know that everything actually is *growing out of control is unclear to me, too, but the fact of it scares me in my bones. The point is that something important will happen when I name the light. The light knows I know its name. The forest knows I know. Everything waits for me to name it, if I could just remember. But I can't.*

1

DAMP CHILL SEEPS THROUGH my jeans from the rotting wood porch stairs of The What Not Shop. There are three places to sit where you won't fall through. I've put in my hours waiting for customers, so I know exactly where to set myself. Green to breathe is everywhere. Ferns up to your armpits and sorrel the size of lollipops poke through the needles and leaves and duff of the forest floor. Redwood trees stand like silent beasts all around, two-cars wide and tall enough to poke holes in the sky. Hurts my brain trying to make sense of that much size and age, eight hundred years old at least, and how they stand so still and silent. Even the sound of my breathing is loud, like I'm some party crasher busting in on an ancient séance, messing with the vibe.

Porch floorboards creak under the weight of Gramps rocking in his rocker that he calls the Throne. One hand grips the arm of the chair, the other wraps around a beer, and a knot in his jeans hangs just below his knee in the space where his leg used to be. He stares off toward the old two-lane highway where the redwoods grow into the road, busting up the edges of the pavement bit by bit, like they've let us borrow the land for long enough and now they want it back.

We sit this way sometimes, he and I.

Three hours to go before my slow-as-sin shift will end and Liza and I can hightail it up to Eureka in her parents' car that she's not supposed to drive. Her parents are away for the weekend, so we're golden. Liza swears the older guys we met last time said to meet them at The Shanty, but I think she's just making it up as an excuse to get us back there. The dude who was into her was supremely hot, so you can't blame her. She fixed her traction-beam-laser-stare on him and sure enough he made his way over to buy her a drink. I swear it's her super power. All she has to do is tilt her forehead down a little, look up and fix her eyes on someone, blink a few times, and curl her lips into a kind of half-smile. Nine times out of ten, and I've counted, the victim does whatever she wants. We get into all the bars that way. "Shhh!" she'll say when she's pulling someone into her orbit. "I'm *magnetizing*." I try to magnetize, but all I pulled into my orbit last time was some guy named Twiggy, which just about sums it up.

There's definitely nothing to magnetize here. Tree-stump sculptures shaped like giant eagles or Bigfoot stand in tight rows in between the shop and the road along with burl tables and chairs and stools made from knobby redwood growths. Gramps's buddies at the mill haul over giant chunks leftover from logs they cut, and some chainsaw artist makes all kinds of hardwood weirdness. Gramps decided trees owed him something after a tree someone else was cutting on a job fell the wrong way and pinned him. It broke his pelvis in three places, broke ribs, and smashed his leg so bad he had to lose it. He used his disability money to buy this hundred-year-old soda fountain turned junk store and tourist trap and set the tree sculptures next to the road. "To lure in the nincompoop city slickers," he said.

It's not right having chopped-up pieces of glossed-over tree sitting in the middle of the last old-growth redwood grove for miles, but I know better than to say anything like that out loud around here. I'm just the lucky hack that works the register after school and on weekends. No one pays me for my opinions. No one really pays me at all, actually. Not that much.

The truth is, Twiggy was a whack job. He pretended like he

was going to kiss my hand like he was a duke and I was some princess and I was all gaga, like I'd actually magnetized something good, but then he shoved my fingers into his mouth and chomped on them and laughed like it was the funniest thing. Psycho. Just watch. When we go back I'll get stuck with crazy while Liza disappears to who-knows-where for who-knows-how-long. I'll do it anyway because the guys in town are dogs or I've known them my whole life and making out with any of them is like making out with your own brother and just the thought of it makes me gag. So I'm Eureka-bound to ace magnetizing. Desperate times and desperate measures and all that.

Or I could go see Peter. There's always Peter.

Uncle Nelson hauls a box out of his pickup from today's run buying up what's on sale at other stores in the area to bring back here to sell. Another one of Gramps's grand plans to make money off of the redwood-gawkers. Nelson tilts the box on its side to maneuver between an outstretched wood wing of an eagle and the arm of a bear, yakking as he squeezes his way through to where we sit on the porch. He won't shut up about who's to blame for the holdup on the logging job he's on.

"Why hold things up so I can't work?" he yells to Gramps. "I'm not making the rules about what gets cut! I'm just bidding on the goddamn jobs trying to make my living! Don't they know that?" He drops his box by my feet when he finally makes it through the wood menagerie. A corner of the box crumples under the fall, but he doesn't care. He's already six beers into Sunday and its only noon.

One at a time I slide back and up the stairs just to get out of arm's reach. Nelson's the kind of guy who punches you in the arm when you least expect it and tells you he's just testing your reflexes. Mine suck. The last punch landed like a super-powered tetanus shot and it was all I could do not to cry. Not to mention that there's an edgy mad in his voice today that feels like it's looking for a place to bust out. Like words won't be strong enough to hold it.

What I hear in the words people say, I swear.

"Since when did working an honest day make me the bad guy?" Nelson spits and tucks a thumb into the pocket of his dirty Carhartts and glares up at Gramps, waiting for him to join in the rant against whoever is trying to stop the loggers from doing their job this time. It's usually crackpot environmentalists suing the lumber companies or hippies sitting in the trees so they won't get cut. Nelson's sure it's the hippies this time. He scratches his head through his bright orange wool hunter hat. Clumps of brown hair poke out from under his hat like sticks.

Gramps takes a long pull on his beer, his one leg rocks him, and his arm crutches dangle on the back of the rickety rocker. "This land is full of the blood and sweat of everyone I know," he says, looking out at the woods like he owns them. The Throne is where Gramps likes to sit and get 'sophical. "I got more time under my belt and dirt in my boots from these woods than a whole busload of those dirtbags combined and they think they know how to take care of the land?" Gramps has it in for the hippies, too.

The sound of a truck reaches us through the fog. Not one single ray of sunshine has managed to break through the heavy gray that sits on Humboldt County like a wet blanket too many days a year. Indian summer should have given us a break already, but it skipped us this fall. The glow of fog lights turns into an old pickup that pulls in and parks.

"How's it goin' Bud?" Gramps yells from the Throne. "Where you hurtin' today?"

Bud hangs on to the car door to haul himself out of the driver's seat. "Hank, Nelson, Jade," he says. Everything about Bud is big and thick—his chest, arms, neck, the skin on his face. Even his eyelids are thick.

This is officially my cue because not only does Bud always hug me for five seconds too long, but he's also a talker and there's no way I'm getting stuck in some conversation about god knows what. Lawn mowers. The extraction mechanism in a dehumidifier. The chicken wire and spit he says he uses to fix every single thing that he has supposedly ever fixed in his entire life.

"Hey, Bud," I yell, careful now to step where the stairs aren't rotten. My escape is so smooth. "Gotta change the record!" Johnny Cash's honey-gravel twang floats from the record player inside. He's shot a guy in Reno for probably the sixteenth time today. *Just to watch him die.* Jee-zus.

The plate glass window reads WHAT NOT across the middle in big, blocky brown letters I painted on when it was slow one day.

"Hey, Bud!" Nelson's voice follows me through the screen door. "What's red and orange and looks good on hippies?" Forever lame jokes.

"What?" Bud says.

"Fire!" Nelson laughs and then coughs. His laugh always turns into a cough.

The round and round of the record matches the round and round of the talk that's just getting started. They beat everything to death. Complaining. Stories. Jokes about hippies that maybe aren't really jokes at all.

Liza and that car cannot come soon enough.

So long as they don't start talking forced extractions and dragging hippies out of the trees, it's all just talk. *Someone's got to put an end to all this*, is what they said before when things got bad. So long as it doesn't come to that.

The old wide-plank floor creaks under my feet, and the fridge motor rattles. Wooden shelves are lined with essentials like chips, onion dip, soda, cigarettes, beer, condoms, "lady things," and tooth-paste. The rest are half full of the crap Gramps buys up—playing cards, shot glasses, extra fishing line and cheap pocketknives made in China that George from the tackle shop can't seem to move.

Cardboard boxes from this morning's run sit unpacked on the floor where Dad dropped them earlier. He took the porch stairs two at a time with three boxes in his arms. Mom curses him for not aging a day since high school except for the little gray hairs at his temples. He's still lean, broad in the shoulders, and no belly yet. "It's a mean day's work," he says about logging every time he's stretched in his worn-out recliner after his shift, "but it keeps me fit."

Nelson watched him work, grabbed Dad's coffee thermos, and poured himself a cup. He took a sip and spit it out on the ground. "Damn it, Stanley, you drink hot oil for breakfast?" he yelled up to where Dad dropped the boxes with a *bang* to the floor.

Dad didn't wait for Nelson's comeback, but cut across the porch and down the stairs to go around back for another load. "I want to be awake during the day, Nellie, not some lollygagging half-wit like some losers I know," he said as he passed. It was too early and Nelson was not caffeinated or drunk enough for fighting, so he wiped his mouth with the back of his arm and mumbled something underneath his breath.

"Is Dad still here or is he out for another run?" I yell to Gramps, but he's so busy getting into it with Bud and Nelson over who to blame that he doesn't bother to respond.

"The holdup could be coming from that corporation down in Texas, Hank. You know that." Bud makes his case to Gramps. "You know they're trying to buy the Skatio Lumber Company and this old town right out from under us. You heard that, right? Well, that's a very real possibility, Hank. We can't assume anything right now."

Johnny Cash sings about how good it is to see the *green green grass of home*, and in a direct beeline out past all their yakking, on the other side of the tree stumps by the parking lot, a group of redwoods stands in a circle. There are ways to get over there without being seen. When the time is right I could slip out the back door, behind the side shed, and it's two steps until I'm smack in the middle of the so-quiet and so-long-alive. Lying there on the soft ground takes me somewhere else. That's all I need to block out all the noise. I swear.

Nelson stands at the bottom of the porch stairs and takes a deep drag on his cigarette. "If those tree huggers want to sit somewhere, then they should go sit on the face of that CEO. Chain themselves right to him. Now *that* might change some things!" Nelson laughs at his sheer brilliance. "I'm gonna get me that bumper sticker. You know it?" Smoke comes out of his mouth in puffs with each word. "It says, 'Save loggers. Cut down hippies.'" He laughs again, his hand still close to his mouth, ready for another drag. He already has a bumper sticker on his car: MISSING: *wife and dog.* REWARD: *for the dog.*

I'm moving back toward the door, slow and easy so as not to be seen, when a kid walks out of the woods, right by my circle of giant trees. He looks like an ant compared to the size of those trees. Brown dreads sit in a nest on top of his head. He has no shoes, holey jeans, a ratty sweatshirt, and a backpack on his back. An empty plastic gallon-sized water jug hangs from his finger and he walks right toward The What Not like he plans to buy something. He could just be a hiker, but I know what kind of math is going on in everyone's head. He's a *fleabag freak* in Nelson's book, the kind that makes life hell for loggers.

A kid like that walking out of those woods. His timing makes me dizzy.

2

NELSON LEANS BACK ON HIS HEELS, crosses his arms over his chest, and watches the kid walk toward us. "You living in those woods?" he yells out.

The kid keeps walking. "Nope." He looks like he's on a mission.

"I'll bet you're not," Nelson says. He walks over to stand between the stairs and the kid. "What are you doing coming down from there then? You know this land is private, right? The state park is miles away."

The kid stops, puts his free hand in the air, and takes a few steps back. "Whoa. I'm just passing through, man." Now everyone is acting like someone is guilty of something. "I'm just going to get a little something to eat, if that's okay with you." Scraggly hairs line the bottom of his chin and jaw. Not much of a beard. He can't be older than me. "I'm just on my way to a trail." The kid tries to walk around Nelson, who steps in front of him again.

"Oh yeah? What trail are you hiking?"

The kid hitches one thumb in the strap of his backpack and with his other hand knocks the plastic water bottle against the side of his leg. "Is it a crime to walk here?" He has no idea who he's talking to.

Nelson shrugs his shoulders. "I guess it depends on where you're walking."

"Look, I just need some water and I'll be on my way." The

kid holds the plastic bottle in front of him like it's proof that what he's saying is true.

"That's an awfully big jug of water for a little hike, don't you think?" Nelson's not giving an inch.

"Oh, forget it." The kid turns to walk away.

I walk to the screen door and stand in the doorway.

"Oh, come on now." Nelson walks toward the kid and puts his arm on his shoulder, buddy-like, like he's going to help him out. "We can help you with some water." He pulls him toward the side of The What Not where the water faucet is. The kid walks with Nelson, looking at him, nervous, and then, just like that, he makes a run for it. He is no hiker. Nelson has an arm on him and pulls the kid back, which makes him fall. Bud is off the porch, standing next to Nelson in no time, both of them standing over the kid.

My heart tries to bust out of the cage of my ribs.

"I don't have anything against you, man! I'm just getting some food." The kid is on his back, looking at them, using his hands to shimmy away, trying to get his feet under his body.

"Not in front of the store," Gramps grumbles, and he shifts in his rocker.

Nelson looks back at the porch and around to the massive trees looking down on us all, like he's heard something and isn't sure where it was coming from.

"Oh yeah. No problem," he finally says to Gramps, and he turns back to the kid. "Just stand up. Come here a minute. I want to tell you something." The kid looks from Nelson to Bud and back again before he gets to his feet. "I just want to tell you something about where to walk." Nelson talks like he's trying to explain something to a dimwit. The kid looks at the ground between Nelson's and Bud's feet, and then he looks right at me. A jolt runs down my spine. His face frozen, eyes wide. Nelson whips his head around and looks at me too. "Do you know him?" Spitting words like bullets. Dad's voice is in my head. *Nelson's six cards shy of a full deck.*

Nelson's dark, mad eyes drill into me. I hold my breath and shake my head no. The absolute wrong thing to do. The kid closes his eyes, his shoulders sag, and he looks to one side, but only for a second before he fixes his eyes back on Nelson, like he's going to stare him down.

Everything is set in motion. I can feel it.

"Yeah. I didn't think so." Nelson turns back around. He puts his arm around the kid's shoulder again and pulls him toward the side of the store. "Come here. I just want to show you something."

"Cripes." Gramps leans over and puts his beer bottle on the porch. He grabs his arm crutches from the back of his rocker, slides a hand in each crutch, leans forward, and swings his one foot to walk. "There's nothing to see here, Jade," he scolds. In three steps he's at the door. I don't know where to be. In or out. I move out of his way. "You best be unpacking these boxes," he says on his way back to his office.

Nelson is on one side of the kid and Bud is on the other. They're telling him not to be stupid, I'm sure, not to hold up the timber sale or get in the way of work. Telling him that he and his buddies should be careful. Telling him about what's happened in this town before, when it got bad. I'm sure of this, but then the kid makes a run for it again and Nelson and Bud are on him, pinning him to the ground. It looks like wrestling, guys goofing off. It isn't.

The kid is the skinniest thing, facedown, his arms and legs flailing, trying not to get caught. Bud sits on top, the mass of him on the kid's back. His hands grab the kid's wrists and wrench them back. Nelson is on his knees, one hand on the kid's head, pushing it into the ground. The kid yelling, "You guys are crazy! I haven't done anything!"

I want to yell for Dad, wherever he is, but I can't find any sound.

"Riley!" Nelson yells back to the mechanic that works on cars behind the store every weekend. "Riley, come here for a minute!" Bud gets to his knees and in one motion stands and then yanks the kid from the ground somehow, holding his arms behind his back. The kid's backpack is still on, his shirt hiked underneath it, his skin pale except for red blotches where he was squashed into the ground. His whole body one muscle. Bud has a serious hold on him. "Riley!" Nelson yells again, and he grabs one of the kid's arms. He pulls, and Bud shoves the kid from sight.

Short breaths come out of me. Gramps knocks something over in the office. I jump. All nerves. They're just going to tell him what's what. That's got to be it. I run to the side of the porch and lean over the railing to see what I can. I don't want to know. There's nothing to see, but sounds get to me. Not words. The kid. Grunts coming from his gut.

Nelson yells, "Pick him up! *Pick him up!*" They're mostly behind the store. Bud hangs on to the kid's legs, laughing. Someone else must have his shoulders. He's kicking wild, crazy as a caught fish. They're just giving him a scare. Nelson walks to the kid's feet. He's holding a chainsaw.

Everything in slow motion.

Nelson puts the saw on the ground and kneels, his knees on either side of the handle part. He pulls a file from his back pocket, leans over, looks closely at the teeth of the blade, and starts to sharpen one.

The kid: *"Please!"* His tiny voice muffled by the heavy damp of the woods.

Nelson doesn't see anything but the teeth of the saw. Not me. Not those guys. Not that kid. He's paying attention to detail. *Dad will stop this.* Nelson sits back on his heels and slides the

13

long, narrow file back into his front pocket. He stands and yanks to start the saw. The sound rips the air. He walks back to I can't see where. The kid's feet kicking to get free. Bud holds on tight, his thick face red. The blade gets caught in something and the kid drops to the ground, feet still.

Nelson cuts the saw and stumbles back to where I can see holding what looks like a raccoon tail in his hands. "I got me a scalp!" he yells, laughing and holding it high, almost doubled over with how funny he is. He stands straight again shakes his score to where the kid is lying. "Tell them how things are around here!" His laugh stops as quick as it started. "Tell them it's just the way we do things." He spits. The guys are laughing. Nelson turns his eyes right on me. He sees I see. "Boys," he yells, staring at me, "I think we caught ourselves a live one!"

I'm all body. Knocking into things. Rocking chairs on the porch. The heavy rock doorstop. The door. My hands open it. I don't go inside. I don't stay outside. Where the hell is Dad? The wonky screen door can't close. In or out. My feet won't decide.

"Jade!" Nelson's voice gets to me from way around back. He's still back there. "Jade!" he yells again.

This is when I disappear.

The needle hits the end of the record over and over. Boxes sit unpacked on the floor. *I got me a scalp!* stuck in my brain. The record player is at the back. My hands lift the needle. Shaking hands. Try to pick up the record by the sides so I don't make fingerprints.

"What are you doing?" The record drops from my hands and lands on its edge with a *crack* on the floor. Nelson stands in the doorway and wipes his hands on a rag. No one else is on the porch. Voices float in from somewhere.

"Nothing." Force myself to talk normal. Fingers try to lift

the record from the floor, but can't get underneath somehow. Pale little uncoordinated things.

"You know him?" Nelson asks again.

There's a chip at the edge of the record and a crack runs all the way to song three. *Screw it.* My foot on the black vinyl; shove my fingers underneath.

"I said do you know that kid?" Nelson talks like I'm the dim-wit now.

The record slides easy back onto the record player. Can't make myself look at him. "Mm-mm." Words will give me away. The needle drops in the middle of the record, where it isn't cracked. There's something behind the counter, underneath on the shelves. I make my way there, move things around like it has to be found—a coffee mug full of pens, a roll of paper towels, two half-drunk sodas, a roll of blank register receipt paper, a plastic tray with paper clips, a mini blue army knife, an open bag of beef jerky. My whole body a pulse. Trying to find the phone. The sound of footsteps. His voice. Me making words. "Yes." And then, "I mean, no." Trying to add things up. *Did he really have a scalp?* This makes me stand up.

Nelson's face is inches from mine, he's leaning over the counter, a red welt swelling above his eyebrow. "We were just playing with him, Jadey. You know that, right?" He sounds like he has marbles in his mouth. Beer stink a cloud between us. Glassy eyes wander slow over my face, like he's looking at me, but also like he's trying to remember something.

"Right," I whisper. It could be true. "Was Dad back there?" I try to speak louder this time. I have to know. I don't move. Making normal. "What time is it?" The shake in my voice gives me away.

"Oh Jadey, Jadey, Jadey," he says, looking down before he reaches over and grabs me at the jaw with one hand, like you

15

would a baby's face you thought was cute, only his fingers dig into my cheek and neck. He shakes my head a little. "Nothing happened, all right?" he whispers. I hang in his hand holding my head, weightless, hollow, dizzy. Brown block letters on the window are backward. TON TAHW TON TAHW TON TAHW. "There was nothing to see!" His eyes widen and he laughs, like he's telling the punch line to a joke. He lets me go. My hands catch me on the counter, lungs suck in air, the grip of his fingers deep in my skin.

"Nothing to see," he says again. "So there's nothing to tell." The sound of his feet, the fridge opening, walking back, a six-pack of beer on the counter. "Right?" Tears drop on my hand. Clench my eyes to stop them falling. "You look like you seen a ghost," he says. Nelson grabs the bottle-opener magnet from where it's stuck on the register. Blood blotch on his arm by his wrist. "Just put it on my tab," he says, and he snaps a lid off a bottle, grabs his six-pack from the counter, and leaves.

He doesn't have a tab.

3

RUNNING UP THE CONCRETE ribbon of road to where Eureka is and where Liza might be. On 101 North. Gulping down breaths. A thousand eyes were on my back when I high-tailed it out of The What Not and I didn't dare turn to look at a single one of them because he saw me see.

No way am I looking back.

Cars whiz by and I drop my Army-green knapsack to the ground that's wet from fog, because I can't get into The Shanty without my ID and where is my ID? One hand digs deep into my knapsack, which isn't even real Army gear. Just fake girly crap with rhinestones that Gramps had at The What Not Shop once. Coins pack the front pockets that only have snaps. I stole them from the spare-change bucket by the door, just in case, the coins we all save for a trip to Disneyland one day. Shoved them in with sweats and stuff. *Like I'm sleeping over at Liza's*, I told myself. Making up stories to keep me on track, but it doesn't even matter because Mom and Lily were out. No one was asking.

My other hand holds the knapsack open, and the empty plastic gallon water bottle from before, the one from the kid, is shoved over my fingers. *How do I even have this?* A drop of water runs down the inside of the bottle and leaves a trail through the moisture trapped inside. Shaking with a shiver like it's Alaska. The knot of sweatpants makes everything impossible so I yank them out and dump them on the wet side of the road. My journal. A pajama top. A toothbrush. Dig around. Untangle clothes.

17

Put them back. Road gravel goes in too. Check my back pocket. My ID is there.

"Nelson *really is* six cards shy of a full deck," is what I'll tell Liza when we're drinking our beers. She'll think that's funny, but I'll tell her, "No. This is *not* funny." And she'll get quiet because I'll be so real and she will feel it. "What *happened?*" she'll ask, and I'll say, "I need a drink." "Okay," she'll say, and she'll leave out what I'll know she's thinking, which will be *You're freaking me out* and *This better be good.* She'll buy me a beer because she'll know that something heavy went down because she knows me like that and because she won't miss a chance to use her new fake ID.

I'll tell her about Nelson and what looked like a raccoon in his hands. *I got me a scalp!* The stink of his beer breath. How he gripped my face like a football and even Gramps walked away. About the kid, wherever he is. Stumbling around? At the cops? Back with his friends? He came out of the woods at exactly the wrong time, that's what he did. He should have played it cool, but he didn't. Johnny Cash shot a guy in Reno just to watch him die. *Jee-zus!* I'll say because Liza and I say it that way. *Jee-zus!* She'll say back. *What else?* But I won't even be able get into what else because where was freaking Dad and did he do this too?

On the other side of the highway, just over the ridge, the whole town of Skatio sits in the middle of wonky, patchwork hills that surround the town, like some crumb stuck in a napkin. Lots of square areas of torn-up and brown clear-cuts sit next to a few squares of older redwoods and lots of other squares with fuzzy, green grow-back. Nothing fits together. A puzzle with wrong pieces.

Not going back home is a tiny awful fact that grows bigger by the second.

Giant trees stand there. "WHAT?" I yell at the trees that

can't even hear. "What the hell do I do now?" The wet of the road bleeds through the knees of my jeans. Wait for an answer because maybe one will come because all kinds of things come to me when I'm around trees. Dad says you can't have a conversation with nature, but that's the dumbest thing I've ever heard. That would be like saying no one ever dreams when they go to sleep. Just because you can't see it happen doesn't mean it isn't real. But I don't go on about things like that. Not in this town. Not even around Liza.

I can't walk around without trees nagging me, like they have a long finger and send it my way. Tap me on the shoulder. I'll have a thought that isn't mine. *Listen, please listen.* I'll stop and wait for more. *Listen to what?* I'll say back because not trying to find out why they're sending all those vibes would be like seeing someone crying and not asking what's wrong.

"Now would be a good time!" I yell again. Tears roll down my cheeks. Thick, gray fog spreads out forever overhead. Breath mixes with moist air, the rush of cars fills my ears, and the trees only stand silent. No help at all. Nature sucks. *Forget it.* Toss my knapsack over my shoulder. The water bottle is something to hold on to. One foot in front of the other.

An old junk of a car pulls over and stops at the stretch of highway on the edge of town. The window comes down. A chick with stringy long hair, a bad dye job turned orange, squints at me from inside. I don't even have my thumb out. "You got any matches?" she asks. Her teeth look like pieces of rotten wood.

"No," I somehow say, and I drag the back of my hand across my cheeks to wipe away tears. Shaking from the inside out.

She turns to the driver, talks something over, and turns back my way. "You can get in anyway." She swings the heavy door open and pulls the back of her seat forward. "Come on," she says. I stare at her, but I only see the kid's feet lying still. "Get in."

And I do because this car is heading north, and north is where I want to be.

The cramped backseat is filled with beer empties, McDonald's wrappers, and wadded clothes piled to my knees. The reek of dirty laundry and stale beer fills my nose. Fabric from the ceiling hangs down low and almost touches my head. Stringy-haired chick heaves the big door closed that creaks as it swings shut, and the car crawls back onto the road.

A guy sits in the back, inches away, propped against his side of the car. A dark hoodie hangs over his head, his eyes closed. His face is the pale blue-gray of the banks of the Eel River when fish and river scum rot on the shore when the water is low from drought. I have never seen a face look like that.

"Don't worry. He's not dead." The chick in the front seat reaches back and slaps the guy on the knee. "Are you, Warren?" she says loud, like she's talking to an old person. "You're still with us, right?" He raises his arm and swats at her, his eyes still closed, moving in slow motion. She slaps his knee a few more times and twists herself farther around to look at me. "He always does this," she says. She stares at me for a second, turns back to the front, and quick as that turns back around again. "My name's Natalie. What's yours?" she says. Her lips are the same color as her spotty, pale skin, and scruffy bangs hang in her eyes that are empty somehow, like no one's home. She could be twenty or she could be forty.

Don't tell her who you are.

A cracked CD case with loopy yellow letters scrawled across the cover is the only thing between Warren and me. I steal a name.

"Mazzy," I say. The word barely leaves my lips.

"Cool," she says, and she turns back around to the front, untangles the sunglasses stuck in her hair, and puts them on her face. A minute later she shifts her glasses back on her head and turns to the driver. "Can we stop for cupcakes? I don't know what it is about cupcakes. Mm-mmm," she says like she's about to bite into one. She digs around in her bag, the glove compartment, under the seat. "Dude," she leans over and puts her face next to the driver man's ear, "I *need* cupcakes."

He says nothing and keeps driving. Natalie digs in her bag again. Driver Man reaches over and knocks her on the head with his knuckles.

"Ow!" she says and hits him back. "What?" He pulls the sunglasses off her head, but they stay tangled in her hair. She grabs them from him and tries to get her hair free. "I know what I'm doing!" she says.

"Really?" He turns to look at her, eyes off the highway, eyebrows raised above the dark of his sunglasses. Crazy brown curly hair is a bed-head tangle, and a red blistery sore marks his cheek above his thick beard. Gray duct tape is wrapped around the forearm of his driving arm like a wide plastic stripe. He picks at a corner of the tape with his other hand.

"I'm just getting organized," she says to the long road. "Is there anything wrong with that?" She waves her hand at him like she's shooing a fly. "Stop looking at me!"

A gag gurgles from Warren's throat and a cough erupts from his chest, but his body barely moves. The two up front don't seem to notice or care, mad at each other, staring ahead. Warren takes a quick, deep breath in before he gets quiet. His chest rises and falls. Still breathing.

My life is a heap of heavy pockets, clothes in a knot, a stiff book, and me speeding in a car with these freaks. I hug my bag tight to my chest like it will keep me from going under, my forehead against the cool of the window, the fog of my breath a circle that gets smaller before it disappears. I breathe it back again. Feeling numb takes over my body and spreads, stealth like a gas. There is the sound of the tires and the rhythm of the road. *Ba-dum. Ba-dum. Ba-dum.*

Something in my chest suddenly grips tight and sends shocks down my arms and legs. *Peter.* I didn't even think of going to him. Breath makes another circle that gets bigger on the window, and I wipe lines in the middle of the fog with the pad of my finger. *BE WITH ME.* As if the letters can connect him to me.

The last of the little company town of Skatio passes by— the giant lumber mill, big and butter yellow, runs right through the center. The Skatio Lumber Company sign sits on top like God looking down on everyone. The grid of company houses, all painted either blah green, pukey beige, or supposed-to-be yellow, look like stale mints, those bad ones in a bowl when you leave a restaurant. Then, in less than a moment, Skatio passes out of sight.

"Hey! Where you headed?" Natalie's voice jolts me back into the speeding car. "Hey!" she says again, and she turns to look at me this time. "You asleep or something? Where are you headed?"

I have no idea where I'm headed. Liza and I should be clinking Bud bottles right now pretending to fight over which song to play at the old juke box so we can secretly decide who's hooking up with what guy.

I didn't see a thing, Nelson, I swear.

Nothing to see, nothing to tell.

The patchwork of ragged clear-cuts stretches out from this side of town too. Everything multiples. Crying hillsides. *I got me a scalp!* The forever war over trees. How Liza and her booty calls always equal me left alone and there's no way I can stomach that. Not today. This day is like the Eel River when it rushes from winter rains. There's no stopping the awful flow of it.

"Where are *you* headed?" I ask.

"Oregon." Natalie stares at me. "Portland." Some of her blowy, orange-blond hair sticks in the corner of her eye, and she doesn't try to wipe it away. "Wanna come? It's ten hours away." She says this in a singsong voice, like she's tempting me with a cupcake or something really good.

Ten hours away. "Portland?" I say, trying it on for size. Ten hours away is safe. Where I can make a plan. It's not forever. "Yeah, I'll go," I say because distance is golden. But Natalie doesn't care. She's already turned back around.

No sooner do I say yeah then Driver Man swerves off the 101 onto Highway 36, which is not exactly the way north, but I keep my trap shut. These guys don't seem like the hack-you-in-to-pieces type, but I'm not about to piss them off. Besides, Driver Man could be using some kind of logic, taking the longest possible indirect route. The 101 is runaway central. Maybe he's just being smart. Maybe he knows something. Maybe he's even looking out for me.

I tell myself this.

The little two-lane snakes away from the coast, along the Eel River, past King Cone, where we go in the summer, the last thing I know this far east. The clammy backseat stink is enough to make me gag, and blue-gray guy gives me the creeps, even though he isn't dead. I breathe through my mouth. My side of the car holds me up, all of me pressing into the seat, the cool of the window against my cheek and forehead, my body easing from the shakes. Settling now. Everything quiet.

There's no turning back.

4

THE WORLD PASSES BY FOR MILES as we drive through old farms and wannabe woods and wide-open spaces. There's grass that needs to be mowed, mailboxes, an old barn, a white fence, a tiny red shed with CARLTON FIRE DEPT. hand-painted in uneven white letters, a field, a gravel driveway to who knows where. Naming what's right in front of my face is like a giant rope I can hang on to that keeps me from the crazies in my head, where I cannot afford to go right now. Monster redwood right next to the road, neon green moss on the bark, bursts of light like electric clouds in the middle of darkest woods, full-on bright when the woods give way to the curve of the Eel.

This is all there is before trees, trees, trees, and more trees, but these aren't even real trees. Massive, dinosaur redwoods that put you in your place are real trees. These are more like those fake trees on the train set Gramps has been building ever since I can remember. Little scrubby things stuck there, like they can be pulled up and moved somewhere else. "Trees are just blades of grass in a big lawn waiting to be mowed," is what Dad says.

I got me a scalp! suddenly rips through my head again like an earthquake. Psycho Nelson's creepy, drunk voice, the feel of his fingers pressed in my neck, like they're written on my skin in permanent marker. I rub at my eyes, my cheeks, my jaw, my neck to wipe Nelson away. Try to stop the replay, but the crammed backseat makes it hard to move.

Do not want to wake Warren.

Natalie rolls down the window and a blast of air fills the car with the fresh of the forest we're driving through and breaks up the stale stink. New air fills my lungs and I shake my head to shake Nelson off of me, drag my fingers down my face, over my jaw and neck and the top of my chest, like I can pull the mark of him from my body and throw it out the window. I do this over and over, but the day repeats itself like an echo.

Natalie's bone-thin arm drops out the window, and her hand rides the air currents like waves. The Eel River still runs along the road and spreads out wide next to us like a little lake. Late-afternoon sun twinkles off the top of the water. Warren's snore is gentle and low. Driver Man whistles three notes, long and slow and repeats himself. Regular trees and skinnier evergreens show up more now. California oaks. Douglas firs. Cedars. A few redwoods here and there, a circle of them right next to the road.

Circles of redwoods are called Family Circles, which I know because Dad tells me about all that stuff in the woods. When a redwood tree dies, new trees grow from the roots in a circle around where the tree once stood. Dad calls the new trees *suckers* or *pecker poles*, but Family Circles is more like it. The trees always look huddled together, their roots like arms around each other, like they're trying to keep what they lost in the family.

I've been hiking to a Family Circle ever since I could escape my house. It's where Peter lives. Rocks and tangled roots make it hard to get in, but once I'm inside the circle, it's the stillest, most quiet, most easy place to be. There is a fire cave at the base of Peter. The wood walls of the burned-out hollow are charred black. Needles on the ground are soft like a bed, tucked in under however many tons of tree still grow tall above the cave. I lie back, and the weight of the quiet squeezes everything out of me. I sink so deep into slow I forget to breathe and wait for the feeling to come.

It starts far off at first, until it comes on strong, and before I know it I'm connected to everything and time. I see things. Not with my eyes, but seeing like dreaming, random things that aren't any random things from my life, none that I remember anyway. More like what trees have seen, a whole story in a flash—a flood that takes everything down, trees the size of trains, drowning, or the time when twelve hundred years old had to learn what it means to finally fall. A neighbor tree leaned more than the wind blows, leaning and leaning until falling. Brown-red bark split into sharp, pointy shards, flying with branches and needles, birds, moss, trunks of trees growing from the main tree with whole worlds in them, huckleberry groves. The way-high top of the tree smashed to bits against another tree hundreds of feet away, everything living and suddenly dying, the earth shaking for miles, louder than one hundred years making its noise all at once. Break-your-heart awful because there was no stopping the massive end of it. So real. But when I opened my eyes it was just me, late for dinner, at the base of Peter with damp duff, roly-poly bugs, and spider webs.

The Here It Comes, I call it. Hyperspace daydreaming with a full-body peace that floods every cell. The best state to be in. I could sit like that with Peter for days. It's just when all the *other* knowing starts rushing in that the problems start. Words lately. Thoughts clear in my head. Ideas way bigger than me that definitely do not come from me that I have no idea what to do with. Lately there's too much of that.

Warren suddenly shifts his body so that he's leaning my way now, slumping almost on my half of the seat. *Please God don't let him kick it and fall over on me.* I hug my body even closer to my side of the car, the cool of the window against my cheek. Natalie grabs random clumps of her hair and braids them, half her head sprouting braids. Driver Man quiet, in a zone.

I let my eyes close and sink into the rhythm of the road. "*One*-little, *two*-little, *three*-little *In*-dians," I sing inside my head, "*four*-little, *five*-little, *six*-little *In*-dians, *seven*-little, *eight*-little, *nine*-little *In*-dians, *ten*-little Indian *boys*." I sing this over and over because what the hell do you do with what trees tell you anyway?

"I know what I'm doing!" Driver Man's voice jolts me awake. We've fast-forwarded to 1-5 somehow, stuck in traffic, the afternoon sun almost down, long shadows and a pinkish sky.

Everything rushes in at once—the dashboard clock reads 6:05; Liza is screwing hotter-than-hot dude, sure that I blew her off, pissed for making her go it alone; Mom's making dinner; Lily's splashing in the tub; Gramps is locking up The What Not. Does anyone even know I'm gone?

1-5 is a parking lot. Driver Man gets off at an exit to try to skip ahead of it all. Everyone else has the same bright idea and we're all in line driving slow together, single file, on a service road along the highway, so slow we could be a parade.

"Not here, man," Driver Man says to the long, standing-still line of traffic. "We can't stop here." He grabs the steering wheel and leans over to the right, looking at the shoulder. He guns it and drives onto the too-narrow side of the road, fast, trying to make it to the overpass. There's a stop sign ahead, and the shoulder gets skinny right by the turn, but this doesn't stop him. He squeezes through somehow and shoots across the overpass. No cars try to block him.

Natalie snorts a crazy cackle. "Wahoo!" she yells as he takes the last turn onto the onramp. Such a jerk move. I'm sure no one will ever let him sneak back in line, but he rides the shoulder until there's a break in the cars and swerves back in like it's his natural place.

We'll get stopped for that, I'm sure. Cops peering in, waving a flashlight, scanning everyone, looking in the backseat, saying, "Wait a minute," going back to their car, sitting there, comparing the perfectly matching description from the radio, coming back, pointing right at me and saying, "Will you step from the car, miss?"

I look around, but no cops are on the overpass. No lights from behind. Yet.

A wide smile spreads across Driver Man's face as he rakes his fingers through his wild hair. "We'll be in Portland in no time." He takes the sunglasses off his face and tosses them onto the dash, where they slide down to the window.

"That was awesome, James!" Natalie reaches over and scruffs Driver Man's hair. He has a name.

"Just checking your pulse, baby." He sighs big before cutting across the lanes to the fast one, where we take off.

Bugs are smacked all over the windshield. I hate the splat of dead bugs. The sky is a crazy mosh of purple, pink, blue, gray, and white. The long road stretches out to forever. Headlights coming at us are a giant string of Christmas lights. The horizon is so far off you can't tell the difference between where the ground stops and the purple, gray sky starts. Eerie sunset quiet feels like the world might just turn itself off.

"You got a place to stay tonight, Mazzy?" Driver Man eyes me through the rearview mirror. He actually talks to me, knows my name. Or my fake name.

"I, ah . . ." I try to find a lie. I have no idea where I'm going to stay. I have never been to Portland. *You're a real whiz!* is what Liza would say right about now. Thoughts start to move in all the wrong directions, back though the day. I skip through the hell parts, black holes I could fall into, and force myself back to this morning. The soft of my bed.

I am so far away from this morning.

"Umm . . ." Hot tears pool in my eyes. I blink hard to keep them damned up, to keep everything from pouring out, but awful thoughts pile on top of each other because now it's a free-for-all.

*Maybe there was no scalp. Maybe it was only dreads. Maybe Nelson
scared the crap out of that kid and didn't really hurt him. What if all
of this is for nothing?*

"Where do we drop you?" Natalie turns back to me again.
Headlights from the car behind us land on her face, and she
squints against the light, trying to see me. Her face is funny,
softer somehow, worried maybe, or waiting for me to say something. Which only makes it worse. She knows how hard it is to
keep it together. Heat flushes from my chin to my forehead. If
I say one word, it's all over. "It's cool," she says after a minute.
"Don't worry about it, Maz." She knows my name, too.

So I do that, try not to worry. Warren's not leaning my way
anymore but is staring out his window. I peel myself off my side
of the car, lean back against the seat, wrap my arms around my
backpack and the plastic water bottle like they're my one and
only teddy bear, and force myself to sleep.

The clock reads 2:30 when we park in front of a trashy little
house at the end of a city block. Everything is dark except for
a circle of a streetlight at the corner and a glowing yellow light
above the door of the house. Portland. James and Natalie talk
in whispers before she heaves the big door open and climbs
out of the car. Cool air rushes in. Natalie crosses the sidewalk,
squeezes through a gate that's falling off its hinges, walks to the
door, and knocks.

"You can hang here tonight, Mazzy." James leans on the center armrest, and we watch Natalie, the still of the car so silent after
hours of driving. "They're cool with people passing through."

The front door opens, and a woman stands behind the
screen, beyond the reach of the yellow light bulb, silhouetted
from behind by the dancing lights of a TV. She's short with hair
piled into a bun on top of her head. She looks past Natalie to the

car and back to Natalie. She shrugs her shoulders. Natalie turns and gives a thumbs-up.

"Get your stuff, Maz," James says as he reaches over to shove the passenger door open. I push the seat forward and toss my girly backpack onto the ground. My empty water bottle lands with a hollow *thump*. Getting out of the hole of the car is a puzzle, god-awful because my bladder is an overripe watermelon in my belly. We'd stopped a few hours ago, but I didn't stretch my legs or pee for fear of being seen.

Natalie whispers loud in the dark as she passes. "She's got a bed you can crash on for the night."

The room with the bed is a cave I can hide in. I hobble to the front door trying not to pee my pants, my too-cramped legs not remembering how to move. A rigged, rickety wooden trellis slants to one side over the cement slab at the front of the door. Next to the makeshift porch is a chipped fake-wood kitchen table with a wooden chair and two plastic milk crates upside down for sitting. "Hey," the woman behind the screen says as she opens the door and steps back to let me through. "I'm Veronica."

"I'm Mazzy." So smooth the way the name rolls from my mouth. A car door slams. Natalie should be hopping in behind me any minute. The rumble of an engine breaks the quiet of the night, and I turn just in time to see the junky car with James and Natalie and Warren drive off. The hot red of the taillights disappears into the dark with what suddenly feels like the only friends I have in the entire world. Desperation is a knot in my throat. "Where are they going?" I try to sound cool.

"I dunno," Veronica says. It's too late for conversation. I didn't even say goodbye. Or thanks for the ride. Standing there, staring after the car, dumb. The smell of curry and incense wanders my way from inside the house. "You coming in?" she says.

The end of the road.

5

VERONICA BANGS ON THE DOOR at seven in the
morning. "You awake, Maz? Want a smoothie, Maz? Actually,
the blender's broken. Did you break it, Maz? Can you fix it?" Her
feet like little shadow bombs under the door.

Day four. Curled in the nest of blankets on the futon on the
floor in this room that is not my room. The horror story jack-in-
the-box that is my life springs up and smacks me in the face: the
rattle of the beer fridge. *Oh Jadey, Jadey, Jadey.* Nelson holding
something. His words dumb drunk mush in his mouth. Breakfast
at my house. Without me there.

I don't make a sound, take in this room in the morning
light, and pray that Veronica leaves soon. A heap of a desk made
of a wood pallet, probably stolen from some grocery store parking lot, sits on top of stacked plastic milk crates. Wooden fruit
crates lie on their side with rumpled clothes shoved into them.
A weird fish-bottle lamp is the only light. Daylight struggles
to sneak through a giant brown tapestry tacked to the window
frame with thumbtacks. Electric aqua blue paint covers half the
wooden trim in the room, the rest left in chipped, midnight
blue.

The shadows from Veronica's feet finally move on from the
slit under my door to who knows where. She's Veroni-witch to
me now because she says she's a for-real witch, but besides burn-
ing a little incense and candles I can't tell what's so witchy about
her. She's more a freak-witch than a witch-witch. And she's a

31

case. Already wants to borrow my stuff and I don't even have any. Walks around the house naked, which is just nasty first thing in the morning. All that body smell when I just want to eat some oatmeal.

Roommate number two is supposed to be a super cool massage therapist, but she spends most of her time at her boyfriend's, so I haven't met her yet. Irina. I can use her room until she comes back. I can pay rent, too, if I stay for more than a week or two. "No problem!" I lied to Veroni-witch. "I have a job," I said, "at a coffee shop." She asked which one. "That one around the corner," I said. Making this up as I go.

There are things to figure out.

My plan for what happens next is overdue. I counted on having at least two or three days before anyone was really worried. Liza would have covered for me for that long if she had to. She'd figure that maybe I'd miraculously hooked up with someone who slipped me his phone number at The Shanty and that I was holed up with him for the weekend. She thinks like that. My parents wouldn't go looking for me for a day or two, maybe even three. They knew I was hanging with Liza. They just didn't know how long. It's the school that keeps track of absence.

I am now officially absent.

And maybe Dad knows exactly why I'm not around.

I have twenty-eight dollars and seventy-two cents. There is a twenty-dollar bill on Irina's desk in a Ball jar with the lid screwed on tight, which I won't use unless I have to. The problem is having absolutely no clue what I have to do. So I stay hidden, mostly, write in my notebook, try to figure what's what and send signals to Peter.

Back home everyone knows that redwood trees have roots that talk to other roots underground. If a tree is sick, it sends *I'M SICK!* through its skinnier-than-thread root hairs, and before you know it a tree all the way on the other side of the grove starts making its own medicine to protect itself. I am so beyond knowing what's what that who knows? Maybe it will work that way with Peter, too. So I test it, from my heart, like a thought that's a pulse: *I HAD TO GO!* I send *IT'S NOT SAFE!* I'm sending one way only though, because if the Here It Comes starts coming back this way, too, it's game over. I cannot handle any extra knowing.

Veroni-witch is loud as a garbage truck from the kitchen to the coat closet to the front door. Five more minutes, just to be safe, and the coast is clear. Untangle myself from the blankets, still wearing the jeans and my dad's old football sweatshirt from high school that I was wearing at The What Not. It's too big and I can cozy into it when I'm sitting there doing nothing. The elastic slides easy from my hair that I finally washed yesterday with the shampoo in the shower. I redo the ponytail that hangs past my shoulders. A little morning air will do me good.

Grab my notebook from under the pillow and the plastic water bottle and slip down the hall to the kitchen that is Pepto-Bismol pink. I fill the water bottle. The supersized Quaker oatmeal still sits on the counter in exactly the same place I left it yesterday. It has kept me going this long without having to go to a market. I haven't ventured that far, not yet, only around the block, which was action enough.

Blur by the mirror at the front door because I can't stand to see myself. The last time I looked my eyes were creepy, green, and hard like marbles with dark breaks on the inside. I duck through the falling-over trellis, and the morning sun is soft on my face. A path winds through the tangle of a yard, and I follow it to a broken cinder block that's jammed into a dirt patch in the corner by the fence, hidden between a giant spiky mountain of rosemary on one side and a huge ratty sage bush on the other. Drop the half-full plastic water bottle and my notebook by my feet and plant my butt on the cinder block. Dry-ish crumbly sage leaves pull off easy, and rubbing sets that crazy green smell free, which floats around my head like smoke after firecrackers. Close my eyes and breathe in deep. *Maybe I'll write you today, Peter.*

The front yard is some kind of vegetable garden that no one has done anything to for ages, so it's a mosh pit of everything growing together, weeds and all. Cleaning it gives me something to do. There's a little patch of weird long grass with blood red tips all tangled with clover-looking weeds and a droopy tree with leaves curling under. I pour water on it from the plastic bottle because it looks thirsty. There is dill that has a Vegas showgirl flower cap with tiny yellow flowers Mom would have pinched off long ago. She said the flower made dill look bawdy. *Bawdy?* Parsley grows long and leggy and has little white flowers that make it look more like a weed than anything else. I pick some of the clover stuff from the blood grass and make a little pile of it at the edge of the bed, but I don't pull too many weeds. Just enough so they don't choke the good plants. Weeds deserve a right to live, too. They're only plants that no one happens to like.

Apron Lady waves from across the street. She was "putting her garden to rest" for the winter when she popped over to introduce herself the first day I was in the garden, clearly checking me out.

"And what do you do?" she asked, looking at me over the top of her reading glasses. She used to work for the city forever, but now she just cooks a lot and always wears an apron over her clothes that reads FBI and has a picture of a target-practice mannequin. The growing-out gray of her dyed dark hair looks like a silvery caterpillar nestled in the part on the top of her head.

"I work at a coffee shop," I said, smiling, staring her straight in the eye, the whole time feeling RUNAWAY branded on my forehead, telling myself *She can't possibly know*. I'm learning how to do this, not give up a thing.

Today Apron Lady doesn't even pretend she's not watching me. She wipes her hands on her FBI apron and heads my way. I ditch the weeds, grab my notebook, and squeeze through the stuck-open gate just as she gets to the curb on her side of the road. "Off to work!" I lie, and I turn down the street without looking back.

Before I can cross the street, Mrs. Johnson spots me from half a block away, standing in her nightgown in front of her house watching me walk toward her. I've met her already, too. "Call me Jo-Jo," she said. "That's J-O-J-O, honey. Short for Johnson." She's got her eye on everything and everyone and talks loud and never stops. You can hear her voice over the traffic from the road. Gave me the lowdown—she has six kids and they all have kids and that's why there are all kinds of people coming and going from her house. She's worked for twenty-two years in the cafeteria at St. Agnes hospital and that's why she can go in and they'll take care of her heart. The lady on the corner hates the people redoing their house on the other side of the block because she thinks the remodel is going to increase her taxes. When Mrs. Johnson pointed to the house on the other side of where I'm staying, she shook her head and said, "Well, I can't even get into that," as if she'd been talking too much dirt about everyone already. Either that or the story was so bad she couldn't repeat it, which made me really want to know.

Mrs. Johnson puts her elbows on the fence, leans over, and yells at her dog. Do not, repeat, DO NOT need to see all that moving around under that thin nightie. "Miss America, get out of that street! Get out of that street!" she yells, looking at me, not even bothering to watch if the pug leaves the road or not. It does. "That damn dog gonna get herself killed one of these days,

I swear by Jesus," she says, and then she points back down the street to where I came from. "How many of you living in that house?"

"Three," I say, which is mostly true.

"Only three of you in that big thing?" The house is not any bigger than any other house in this neighborhood full of funky little houses, most falling down, except for a few that are being rebuilt fancy this time around.

"Only three," I say as I pass. The less I say the better.

"Hmph," she says, and that's it.

When I met Apron Lady the first time, she told me that she never ever wants to deal with Mrs. Johnson because she's worried she's going to come asking for money, which I guess already happened once. Only it wasn't Mrs. Johnson who came asking for money, it was her granddaughter, who she calls Mother because the girl is so bossy. Mother gave the Apron Lady a note from Mrs. Johnson asking for money. The Apron Lady hasn't decided yet how she is going to deal with the situation. Mrs. Johnson hasn't asked me for money yet, which is a good thing because I don't have any to give her and who knows what will happen if I say no.

There's one other lady around here I can't quite figure out—an older, sporty-looking lady with chin-length gray hair. She's been in Mrs. Johnson's yard with a little dark green plastic wheelbarrow and a hand shovel. She walks to the block behind us with her wheelbarrow. She walks in the alley behind the house. She walks real slow and stops and stares into the yard. Sometimes she'll stand there for five or ten minutes staring. I really want to know what she's doing.

The city grid of North Portland is full of right turns. At the corner, I have to turn right because I can't turn left, which would take me back toward Apron Lady. Turning around is not an option. Going straight would only turn into wandering, and my whole body gets exhausted thinking about all that time on my hands with nowhere to be and nowhere to go. The fact is I have a room with a door on it and that's where I want to be, right now, with the door shut.

Halfway down the block is the turn for the alley that runs behind the houses, a shortcut. The alley is junk. Scratchy greens are sometimes taller than my head, and a skinny trail runs through the little city jungle. Pray it's too early for drug deals and smack freaks. There's a leftover car with weeds growing all around it. Little backyards sit quiet and empty without whoever lives there poking around in them. Piles of full garbage bags wait by a back gate, an outdoor table holds last night's party, sidewalk chalk lies at the unfinished part of some kid's picture, and rolls of rusty chicken wire sit next to a random toilet. When I get to my place, I pull back hard on the broken chain-link where I'm staying, make myself skinny enough, and start to slip on through.

My hood gets caught on the fence, and I try to unhook myself, but I'm hitched at a weird angle. Drop my notebook to the ground so I have two hands free, but there's rustling in the weeds. I stop moving and hold my breath. The littlest move jangles the fence. Tall grasses twitch, and I'm stuck, ready to punch or kick at whatever's coming for me. Out of the back-alley weed riot, Miss America pushes her furry round face that looks like a burnt pancake.

She walks right by where I'm all knotted, like I'm holding the fence open just for her. She gets inside and kicks dirt with her back legs that shoots across the yard before she squats low like she's going to poop. I yank myself hard off the fence and run crazy after her for scaring me, but she's too fast and her corkscrew curly tail disappears around the house.

By the time I make it around front she's already planting her butt again, staring at me, ears bunched in wrinkles over her eyes. I'm ready to kick her out of the yard, but then I stop. Is dog poop the same as cow manure? At home, in the spring, when I walk around town, I can tell by the smell which yard gets chicken poop or whatever kind of poop isn't cow manure. Of course I have no cash to give this garden any poop, but maybe Miss America can be my own little personal fertilizer.

A guy walks to the gate holding a parsley plant with roots hanging from the dirt ball. No pot. Just a plant with roots like he just dug it up. He holds it in front of him. "You want some parsley?" He smiles. "I bet you love parsley."

From poop to parsley.

His smile is yum. I really should get back in my room and shut the door, but my notebook in the backyard with too much top-secret information in it pops into my head. "Hold on," I say, "I'll be back in a sec."

I run back and grab my notebook, and on my return to the front I trip on a rock that's hiding in the weeds and nearly face-plant by the cinder block. My notebook flies to the ground.

"Ooof," says the guy still standing there. "You okay?" He is skinny, all bones and shoulders and tall. His hair is golden brown, curly and kind of long. His eyes are big and green and a little buggy. His smile is smooth lips and straight white teeth. Sure he's skinny, but he is no Twiggy. The kind of guy Liza would try to magnetize. The parsley hangs from his hand, still on offer. For me.

I don't know what to do with myself. "Yeah," I say. "I'm cool." There's a small head of what I think is lettuce in the mosh pit garden, and suddenly it seems like a good idea to make a trade. I snap the knot of leaves off at the base and hold it like a skull by the hair and offer it to him. He takes it. I take the parsley. I sit back down on my cinder block. He eats the lettuce. We don't talk. A dumb, cute grin lights up his face as he swings one foot back and forth, trying to balance himself, but he keeps knocking himself off-balance. He eats the whole head of lettuce.

"My name is Justin," he says when he's done, and he wipes his mouth with the back of his arm. "What's your name?"

"Mazzy," I say. Apron Lady watches from her spot in her keeling-over sunflowers.

"Cool name," he says. His gray-black RAMONES T-shirt looks two sizes too small.

"I picked it," I say, proud of my new name, but as soon as the words leave my lips I could kick myself because that's just the type of thing to say if you want someone to ask more questions, like, *Why'd you pick it?* or, *Where'd you pick it from?*

"Where are you from?" he says instead.

Of course it would come to this. "I'm not from Portland," I say because I seem to be losing my head because he gave me some parsley. *Idiot.* Why didn't I say something simple, like, *I'm from here*, or, *Who cares where?* My absolute dumbest move yet sends shockwaves from my gut to my skin, but I play it cool.

"Well. Where *are* you from?" he asks again. "Canada?"

This is all my fault. "No." My brain is jammed.

"New York City?" He says *city* like "sit-*tay.*"

"Nope," I say, and for some reason no places come to mind. Panic rises in my chest.

"Idaho?" He sounds pretend frustrated, like he's about to give up. The green in his eyes is like olives.

"Yes!" I say just to change the subject. "That's it! I'm from Idaho." Flipping Idaho.

"Ah." He starts to swing his leg again, and a devilish grin spreads across his face. "I don't think so," he says. "You know, I know who you are. I've been watching you."

"Oh yeah?" I kind of whisper because I cannot find any

sound. He could have been speaking French. "What?" What did he say, exactly? I can't breathe. *How could he know?* "What did you say?" I say this I don't know how many times.

"You're from Greece," he says.

Greece. If I hadn't been sitting down, I would have needed to. Sitting, clammy, catching my keep-it-together breath. I slide the ponytail holder from my hair. I put my ponytail back in, smoothing back every single hair on my head, over and over.

"This is how I figure." Justin crosses his daddy-longleg arms across his chest and points a dangly finger at me. "I've been watching you in your garden. Cute alterna-girl down the street who writes in her journal and happens to really dig plants. But today you weren't just watering the plants. You lunged in and actually spent time with them. I saw it." He pokes at the air like he's making an important point. "And you know lunges originated in Greece. I am sure of it. During the original Olympics, when early runners experimented with ways to stretch their muscles." He's on a roll, walking back and forth next to the falling-down fence. "And this gesture, which is frequently expressed by your body, must come from an ancient knowledge inside you. Probably not from the Olympics though, but from some Bacchanal ritual of which, one of your lifetimes ago, you were absolutely a part of. It is completely clear from the way you relate to parsley, and for that matter rosemary, that you must have been Greek and most likely a goddess of some stature. That's why I gave you the parsley plant. Don't you see?"

What I see is that he's stoned and has no clue where I'm from. I am not busted. And he's cute as sin and wants to talk to me and called me a goddess and Liza's not here to steal my thunder and he gave *me* something and I'll take it, roots and all.

My full-body panic starts to drain down through my feet as I wander around weightless, giddy from not giving myself away.

I pick pieces of vegetables from the garden and give them to him one at a time while he eats them and tells me all about their origin. Justin can talk Veggie Latin to me forever for all I care if I can feel all this rush in me. Like life is normal. And it makes the missing less. Which it does, for a little while. I just have to keep my head.

6

VERONI-WITCH HAS AN ANCIENT CAT named Tater, and fleas are feasting on him. And I don't know what happened, probably just old, but his back legs don't work. You can hear him coming down the hall. His front feet make a *thump-thump* sound before he drags the back half of his body. *Thump-thump drag. Thump-thump drag.*

The worst part is that he can't scratch his fleas because his back legs don't work. He props himself on his front legs, tilts his head to one side and shakes it a little, and just stares at you like, *Will you please scratch my head for me?* I'm not mean, but I can't bring myself to do it. I love animals. Had kitty twins Peanut Butter and Jelly, but it's just all those fleas and flaky skin and old hair. Jee-zus. Can't do it. He looks like he's counting *1, 2, 3*, and he whips his back legs toward his head to try to get a good scratch in somehow, but he manages to flip himself over.

Mornings are hell with Tater sitting desperate in the middle of the kitchen and Veroni-witch flying around naked, making breakfast, saying *poor Tatey*. She even holds him against her naked, and feeds him these crazy cat vitamins called Artichoke Micro-Clusters. She goes on about how she'll never bomb the house because of chemicals and whatever, which would be fine if the cat was actually mostly alive. She even wants to have a house meeting about it and told me I have to come, which I guess I have to because how can I not, crashing at this place for free.

Ten days now. I've driven right off the map of my life on a one-way street and there's no place to turn around. I can't find my way back.

It's just after midnight and sleep is not happening because the old mismatched flannel sheets on Irina's bed are infested. A whole flea tribe is having a massive party, and I'm the party food. I haul my sorry butt out of bed, shove my notebook way under the mattress so Veroni-witch can't find it if she comes snooping, and I sneak out to my secret spot on the cinder block.

The front yard is a mess. It looks like my hair did when I was a baby. There's a picture of me with tufts of hair and lots of bald patches all over my head. For some reason clumps of hair fell out before my real hair grew in. I looked a little sick and now the garden does too. I thought I was making a dent, but there are random bald spots and piles here and there where I'd pulled up a few weeds at a time, moved to another part of the yard, pulled up some more, and just left them on the ground.

The rattle of wagon wheels grinding the sidewalk breaks the silence of the night. I hunch to stay hidden, find my way over to the fence, and peer over just in time to see the lady with her wheelbarrow passing. The wheelbarrow has plants in it, and she is walking down the street regular, like it's daytime. Little baseball cap on, garden gloves even, like she's going planting. The triangle tops of the wooden fence poke into my palms as I lean over to watch where she goes. When she gets ahead to the next block, I squeeze through the garden gate even though I don't have shoes. I have to see what she's up to.

Tiptoe which is dumb because she is so far ahead and there's no way she can hear me, but there's glass and god knows what else to watch out for. Pass Mrs. Johnson's house, and she's right that there's all kinds of people coming and going from her house, hanging on her front steps. Farther up some spray-painted yellow car is parked. The little car looks like a joke, but up close the deep bass *dom dom dom* and creepy green stenciled letters on the side that say NO MERCY make it no joke. The window rolls down as I walk by. Smoke sneaks from the car and some guy watches me. Scary, evil eyes. I keep walking, faster now, and set my sights on Justin's house where the TV's on, but the curtains are all pulled tight. Dark. All these houses with people doing their night thing. The air smells like summer turning into fall.

The lady, who is Garden Lady to me now, turns on to MLK Boulevard and only goes about two blocks, stops her cart, and gets down on her knees. She's in the stretch of blocks where no stores or bars or anything is—a bus stop, some old car wash that doesn't work anymore, a lot with weeds, a building they're either building up or tearing down, I don't know which. I pull a newspaper from the weekly paper bin and lay it on top of the bin and look like I'm serious about finding something. Maybe even news from home that's made it all the way here. COMPANY TOWN FALLS TO CORPORATION or LOGGING TOWN TURNS VIOLENT AGAINST PROTESTORS. It wouldn't be the first time, but there's no news like that. I read movie listings instead. *Two Thumbs Up!* Not that Garden Lady would know.

I'm in a good position because I'm in between streetlights. She can't see me. I can kind of see her though, and she's busy with something on the ground. This makes no sense because it's all concrete. *Breathtaking! Astonishing! See It!* I want to get closer, but I don't dare. Maybe two cars whiz by. Mostly it's quiet with nighttime city noise.

Garden Lady looks my way quick, stands, and leaves her stuff on the ground. She walks over to the bus stop and sits down. What, so now she's going to wait for the bus? She sits there, looking regular. And, just like that, the bus comes flying down MLK. It's like she knows the schedule or something.

Spectacular! It's So Rousing You May Hardly Be Able to Contain Yourself!

Garden Lady pretends to be reading. There's that weird decompression sound when the bus opens its doors, the light from inside glows in the dark, a tin can floating bubble of light. She's *not* catching the bus. Where did her book even come from? The bus bubble floats on, and Garden Lady goes back to work. Is anyone else catching all this, in some random apartment above some old store, awake too late with nothing better to do than watch what's happening on MLK?

She's back down on her knees, gets busy, stands, moves down a few feet, goes back down on her knees, gets busy again, and repeats this maybe five times. Finally, she goes to her cart, picks up some flowers, and plants them. Can flowers even grow in concrete? She must have had some kind of drilling tool to get through it. I stand at the weekly paper bin shivering in twitches because dork me only has Irina's little T-shirt and jammie pants on, but I don't care. My mind is so blown.

When she's done, she stands, grabs her cart, and pulls it toward home on the other side of the street. I don't move because I don't know which will call more attention to me, just standing there reading the paper at like one in the morning, or moving, which might catch her eye. I wait while she walks, trying to see across the street into the ring of light made by the streetlight by the bus stop. When she turns back onto our street, I cross over to look at her handiwork.

There are perfect round holes a few feet across in the concrete, which must have been put there by whoever made the building for some bushes or something. They'd been forgotten about long ago. But there, in the middle of dirty street crud, is fresh, dug-up earth and maybe fifteen flower plants. I can feel their fragile stems and papery petals in the midst of all the hardness that surrounds them. They speak to me. HOPE they say in what used to be dumpy, empty, litter-filled flowerbeds. I want to cry for what Garden Lady has done. These flowers will change the day of every person who walks this way. Simple as that.

The middle-of-the-night chill gets to me, and I start to make my way home. If Liza were here, she'd say, "Dude! That lady was a crazy person!" But I know better. She's busy fixing a world that no one else can see. I try to decide what Garden Lady's superhero name should be. Flower Power? That's old news. Spring Eternal? Hallmark-card silliness. Concrete Jungle Transformer? Too many words.

I'm sure Justin would have a good name, and just as this thought happens in my head, I swear I hear a voice that sounds like a loud whisper. I stop and look around for where the voice is coming from, praying that it isn't just in my head. That's when I see him. Long, lean, lovely Justin sitting on his porch steps plucking away at his guitar that is missing strings. "It's the Garden Goddess!" he whispers again.

"Why did you say that?" I whisper back from where I stand on the sidewalk, wondering how Justin could possibly know about Garden Lady and what's she's done and the name I'm trying to choose for her.

"Because that's who you are!" he says without whispering this time and his yummy, silly grin spreads all over his face.

Justin is calling *me* the Garden Goddess, which is the second gift he's given me. I will never give the title to Garden Lady even if she is way more of a superhero than I'll ever be.

Liza would be so jealous.

I walk over to where he is on the porch, feeling like everything has some kind of preset alignment. "If there were a superhero lady who turned cities into amazing gardens, what would she be called?" I ask him.

He stops playing for a minute, and his swimmy green eyes look to the night sky. He scratches his chin with his pick and looks at me. "Verde Eruptus," he says, which, I don't know, maybe it could work. "Come here," he says and stands, holding his guitar at the neck. "I have something to show you." He grabs my hand, and the soft, warm of his skin startles me. I don't want to let go. We walk around the side of his house in the dark of the night. "No, wait," he says, and he stops just before we get to the backyard. "Close your eyes." When I do, he pulls me forward. "Just a little farther." Clumps of grass make me stumble. "Ta-da!" he finally says. "Now you can open them."

The grandest old Doug fir that I have ever seen stands alone in the yard, all one-hundred-plus years of him. *Like you, Peter, but not.* There are a lot of trees stuck in odd places in the front- and backyards of houses in some parts of the city like leftovers, but this one has the room of the whole backyard, branches reaching into the other yards. I am so happy it knows nothing about fences and property lines and the end of one space and the beginning of the next. It simply reaches up and out and down all at the same time because that's what it does.

"What's with the tears?" Justin asks, and I don't even know I'm crying. I do know, but I can't stop. There's so much I want to tell him—how much the Doug fir reminds me of Peter and back home. How I had to leave. About the kid at The What Not and how he was really hurt, or worse. How maybe the cops are looking for witnesses. I am one of them. How maybe my dad was part of it and my uncle is psycho. How Nelson knows I know and will never, ever let me forget it. I want to tell him that I only have fifteen dollars and forty-six cents left before I have to break into the Ball jar on the desk. How maybe even Liza is worried by now. How not being able to go home is a non-stop knot ache. The fact of it hurts in my bones. But I can't say a word of it. All I can say to him is, "What a great tree."

The beautiful, always-there tree stretches to the sky and wants me to come over to it, which I do and don't want to do. Justin drops his guitar, puts his hands on my cheeks and uses his thumbs to wipe the tears. "Oh," he says. "It's the magnificent mad, sad, glad, isn't it?" And he's right. It is.

He wraps his arms around me, and his soft flannel shirt smells like campfire. He picks up his guitar and walks me over to the tree, and I let him. We sit down and lean back and everything in me falls into the wood body of that old Doug fir, and it holds me. Just like home. Justin leans back, too, and starts to pluck a tune.

The soft sounds of his melody float around us, and I close my eyes and see Lily's round cheeks and soft, dark, curly hair. Little sister sweet pea. She likes when I take her to where Peter lives. We climb inside the circle of trees that she calls the Circle of Giants, and we lie back on the bed of needles, side by side because there isn't much room. She always takes my earlobe and rubs it between her fingers. Such a funny, weird, Lily thing to do. She does it to all of us. We barely notice anymore. Our ear lobes are like her little cozy blanket.

Lily always wants to hear stories. Her favorite is the one when we lie on the back of the sky-high hawk and fly over the redwood forest where we live. I've told it to her at least a hundred times. It's one of the things that I'd seen when I was with Peter one day. I let myself go dreamy, deep inside the Here It Comes, when suddenly I was on the back of a giant bird flying over the forest. It felt so good to be carried and tucked into the feathers. Who knows where we were flying. I didn't even care. I sang to myself, some odd little tune, and rested. The sound of voices reached my ears, singing mixed with mine, but so quietly I wasn't even sure it was there. I held on to the bird's feathers and leaned over to see if I could find where the voices were coming from.

"It's the trees," the bird called back to me, but they looked like regular trees. They didn't look like they were singing, whatever that looks like. "And it's the grasses and the river," the bird called again to where I sat nestled between its wings. "The world sings with anyone who knows the song." The sweetest feeling filled me from head to toe knowing that I wasn't singing alone. "We just wish that more of you knew the tune," the bird said as we flew. "We'll keep singing until all of you do, but *you* have to keep singing, too! Promise you'll sing!"

Lily always interrupts the telling because she likes to describe everything she sees from way high up, like she is on the bird, too. "There's our house and the eucalyptus tree swing at the river bend where's it's so mucky. Look, Jade! I'm swinging! And, over there, that's school!" Her eyes closed as she pictures the world.

"I hear it too, you know!" she whispered one day when I was telling her the story, mad like I was dumb for not thinking that she could hear the song, too. "I hear the grass singing," she whispered with her little-kid lisp. "And the grasshoppers and the fish and the banana slugs and the needles and the ferns." She sang a made-up tune that sounded so tiny in those giant, wet woods. I hummed along with her, until I whispered that it was time to go.

"Damn it!" she said loud and broke the spell. She's always cursing.

But now here I sit. The tree at my back with the impossible web of a car horn and a dog barking and a plane and cars and Justin's breathing and his strumming and someone's radio or TV and the in-my-heart thump of some cruising car's *dom dom dom* bass wondering if it's stupid NO MERCY I'm feeling. Lying on all this sound like a hammock, rocking here. So far from home.

I can't believe I left Lily behind.

7

SITTING ON MY CINDER BLOCK making a plan to de-riot this crackpot garden that needs room for the sun and water and air to swirl all around so that it no longer feels all stuffed together. The garden is like a continent without a color-coded map that shows you what countries are where. I'm pretty sure there are individual states in there, like the State of Broccoli and the State of Chives. That's pretty clear because of the punk-rock purple flowers. There's the State of Something Green and Red, which could be beets. And there is just the general State of Things, which could be weeds, but could be something and most likely is many things. I hope it is lettuce and zucchini and cucumbers and carrots. Hard to tell. Who plants vegetables and doesn't pick them, but just let's them duke it out with the weeds?

I'm sitting with the Veggie States when Veroni-witch comes flying from the house, yelling, "What are you doing?" Like I poured weed killer all over everywhere within a mile of the house. Way too upset. "You're late for the house meeting!" she says. Which, of course, how could I forget?

Inside is arranged with incense, candles, and a circle of pillows on the living room floor. Veroni-witch, who is now v-w to me, says, "I'd like us all to put some energy into seeing money come to me."

"Us all who?" I say, which is a reasonable question since there are only two of us in the room.

"Well, Irina is supposed to be here, too," she says, and she points to the third pillow. Irina came home for about a minute the other day to grab some of her things before going back to her boyfriend's. "Anyway," v-w twirls some of her long brown hair near her ear. "It's not so much just the money, but I know that I am meant to be following my path, and what I need to see is how to be on my path. I know once I'm on it, there will be, like, total abundance. I know I am a healer and without money I can't truly dedicate myself to that." All of this from a tiny witch with only her underwear and a skimpy tank on. "Close your eyes," she says.

"I thought we were going to talk about the fleas," I say, pushing my luck because its almost three weeks now and she hasn't said anything about paying rent.

"Shhhhh!" She shhhhhh's me. "Oooommmmmm. Oooooomm. Oooooooomm."

I sit quietly, god knows why, but mostly because this is too unreal. I so want to laugh and I totally would if Liza were here because she would not be able to take one single second of this and would do something like put her hands up to her mouth and blow a fake fart when v-w's eyes were closed and then look innocent like she didn't even hear anything. She makes me pee sometimes how funny she is.

v-w is deep into her trance. I close one eye, but I keep the other eye on watch. There's a distinct possibility that Tater is going to try to crawl into my lap now that I am sitting on the floor, and my skin is already in shreds from scratching at flea bites. He is not welcome anywhere near me. Five painful minutes pass, maybe more, and v-w really can sit that way for that long.

"What are you getting?" she asks suddenly.

"Me?" I say, but then I answer myself in my head, *No, Irina*, which cracks me up. v-w is so in her state that she either doesn't notice or is ignoring me.

Her eyes open quick, like she's possessed. "Mazzy, what are you getting?"

"Me? Um. I'm getting that you should get a job."

She freaks on me. "What do you mean? That can't be right!"

Now I am truly scared. "Um. Just, you know, a little one," I say.

"Well, I can't do that," she says, and she starts pulling long clumps of hair from around the back of her neck and ties them under her chin.

I'm about to say, *The world is trying to tell you something and you're not even listening!* But before I say it, something inside of me gives way and I'm hollow, empty, and breathless because I suddenly know that message is meant for me. I stood in front of a payphone for at least an hour yesterday like some lurking goon trying to get up my nerve to call Liza, but I finally turned away. I couldn't handle news from home. I just didn't want to know and didn't want to put her in a bind. It's *me* who's not doing what I know I should. This knowing goes right through me, a bug pinned to a board, stuck there.

There is a knock on the door, which is a huge thank god, because v-w's head is about to spin and so is mine. v-w opens the door, and Justin's voice comes from behind it, which only makes matters worse. I want to sneak into my bedroom without being seen. It's been days since I left without saying goodbye when the night turned so weird.

Justin and I had been cuddled up next to his tree when tingles started at my fingertips and I began to feel a little dizzy and dreamy. I know this feeling too well, so I leaned away from the tree and said, "I'm cold," to keep the Here It Comes from coming on because it's hard enough to keep my head without all that in the mix.

"Well, let's go inside," Justin said, twirling his fingers in my hair. I was tweaking because this is a city after all and the Here It Comes only comes on in the woods, or so I thought. I was not expecting it. I stood. "Don't go," he said. "You can sleep over if you want." He was so yummy I thought maybe it could be a good thing. Rest in sleep.

"Let's go then," I said, and I nearly ran in through the back of the house just to get moving. The kitchen light attacked my eyeballs, and it took a few moments to adjust. There was a bright yellow tablecloth with a knitted centerpiece that looked like grapes. The table was set, and each place had a tiny glass animal at the top by the fork.

"My roommate is a little whacko," Justin said when he saw me eyeing the table. "C'mon." He motioned for me to follow him down the hall, and I did, figuring I'd just lie down, close my eyes, and turn it all off, even though all I really wanted to do was eat him.

Justin had nothing in his room but piles of books, clothes on the floor, a small dresser, and a lava lamp that gave the room an orangey glow. He plonked his guitar in the corner and crawled onto his double bed that is two mattresses stacked on top of each other on the floor. I crawled into bed and made a deal with myself: *We can sleep together, but not "sex" sleep together. Only "sleep" sleep together.*

Before I knew it his lips found mine, and he was the best thing I had ever tasted. But we were not "sex" sleeping together, so I forced my head to find the flat of his chest and nestled in there even though it took every ounce of my willpower. Justin's fingers twirled around my ear, and he didn't say a word. Bonus points for him. We laid together in the orangey dark, our breathing rising and falling, drifting off.

Then the old dream begins again: I stand in a forest under an inky dark sky. An oak tree looms before me with thick, snaking branches that kink and bend and grow right before my eyes.

Light glows from the tiny tips of each branch, the whole tree a glowing silhouette in the darkness. I have one single job: to name the light. I've had this dream so many times before. I made myself stop having it because I can never remember the name, but this time is different. The name is on the tip of my tongue. My heart is pounding even in my sleep.

"Hey, Maz," I heard in the dark, "my tootsies are cold!"

My eyes flew open and I stared at Justin. *Your flipping feet are cold?* His room in the morning light was somewhere I've never been, and he was already back to sleep just like that. I missed the chance to know the name. I was half-asleep and crazy for not knowing, but I climbed out of bed and found Justin his socks because if his freaking feet were cold, and he woke me up to tell me that, and I was now completely awake, then he wasn't going back to sleep either. I went right to the right drawer, which how did I know? I threw the sock-ball at him.

"What's wrong?" he said. Stupid, cute, sleepy face.

The morning horrors jack-in-the-box sprang at me like they do every morning now. I had to leave before I turned to a ball of blubber and snot.

"What's wrong, Maz?" Justin asked again. That's not even my name. I picked up his clothes and threw them back down.

"Nothing," I said. "I have to go to work." His sleepy eyes were on my back watching me not be able to find anything. "Nothing's wrong," I said again because the quiet was loud. "Do you even have a job?" I don't know what he does. I don't know if he works or is in school. He told me he was a student of life, but whatever. I was down on my hands and knees and my sneakers were under Justin's dresser. I sat on the corner of his mattress with my back to him while I pulled at my laces. "Nothing's the matter, all right? I just have to go to work." So tired from not being able to ever get away.

"All right. Good luck with that," he called after me. I left without turning around or saying goodbye because tears were dropping from my eyes like bombs.

But that was a few days ago and now Justin stands in the doorway, the light from outside glowing around all his tall and v-w and all her small and I want to remove her from the picture. I feel lame for being such a walkout loser, but then I am not so sure I feel bad at all, because what is he doing here if he isn't here to see me?

"I'm here for my smoothie!" he says, looking good enough to eat.

v-w starts snuffing the candles. "Well, this house meeting is over now. I have a client." Client? "Whatever you got about a job, Mazzy, can't be right because I already have one. I sell spirulina algae." v-w has not been honest with me. Some pyramid scheme or something.

v-w drags Justin into the kitchen and, cute puppy that he is, he whispers when he walks past. "Do you want to hang tonight?"

I'm pathetic. Of course I do. Soaking in Justin's smile that he's sending my way. "Maybe," I say, and I send him *Be with me* vibes.

When they're in the kitchen, I go to the back porch and sit on the top of the stairs so I can spy. v-w is still prancing around in her undies and little tank top. She's round in all the right places. I'm round in only weird places. One. Most of me is lanky, but I've got a little belly that pooches out. I could be a kangaroo.

"What is spirulina?" Justin acts genuinely interested. "Where does it come from? What does it do for you?" v-w hands him his spirulina smoothie. She has obviously had hers because she has a spirulina-smoothie mustache, all sea-monster green above her lip.

I have to look down because I hear *Thump-thump drag. Thump-thump drag.* Coming right to my feet. We're outside so it's okay, but Tater makes the mistake of looking up at me. God it's awful because when he looks he tilts his head too far back and somehow it makes him fall backward down the stairs. *Ba-da-bump, ba-da-bump, ba-da-bump*, down he goes until he lies at the bottom of the stairs. I think for sure he's kicked it and I run down to see. He isn't all soft and lazybones like most cats when you hold them. He is stiff and hard. Poor thing. I run him back up the stairs and in on Veroni-witch smoothie lip in the kitchen, where I lay the poor cat on the floor.

I'm pissed now. "He fell down the goddamn stairs, Veronica!" Way over this whole thing.

"Oh, Tatey!" v-w plunks her glass in the sink and talks like she's talking to a baby, like he stubbed his toe or something. She lifts him from the floor. "Oh, he's okay. Aren't you, Tatey."

"Why don't you put him out of his misery?" This blasts from me louder than I expect it to.

v-w acts upset, like the cat shouldn't hear anything like that. "If Tatey wants to go, he'll talk to me, and he hasn't said anything yet!" She looks at me like I am evil.

Justin watches all of this. "Um, yeah," he joins in. "He's been talking to me, and I think he might be ready."

Veroni-witch rolls her eyes at us and stomps to her room with Tater, as if we're the ones who let him break his poor back falling down all those stairs.

Yummy J has to leave to take a bike back to his friend's house. On his way to the door he asks if we can hang again. "Yeah, maybe, in a little while," I say, playing it so cool. Really what this means is that I'm just a little while away from *mmmhhhhhhmmm*.

8

CRUISING DOWN THE SIDEWALK on one of J-man's bikes when Garden Lady turns the corner and is suddenly walking my way. We have one of those dorky, almost-crash moments because we both try to be nice and let the other person go first, but we both go first on the same side of the sidewalk and I almost run her over. She dodges me at the last minute, and I don't crash into her wheelbarrow with her precious plants. I run into a car instead.

She asks if I'm okay, which I am, and she's about to keep going when I say, "I've seen you around!"

"Yes," she says. "I'm in the neighborhood." Garden Lady face-to-face! There is so much I want to ask her, but instead of finding words, I don't know what to say.

She smiles and starts pulling her little wheelbarrow o' goodness away, so I say the first thing that comes to mind. "You really like plants, huh?"

She stops and turns around. "Yes," she says, "I do." She's older. She could even be a youngish, sporty granny. I peek into her wheelbarrow wondering where all those little beauties are going to land—in front of Safeway on the busy corner? In a median strip? Maybe in the front yard of that house that caught on fire that no one seems too interested in since it's mostly burned, sitting there all charred.

Garden Lady doesn't seem like she's trying to get away now, but she doesn't say anything, either. Waiting for me, maybe. She must have seen me that night reading the paper on MLK. Maybe she's worried that I'm going to bust her. I smile hard and keep looking at her plants.

"I see you've been trying to clean that vegetable garden you inherited," she finally says, because I'm standing there like a silent loon. I tell her it's like a continent without a map. I don't know why I say things like that. "You've got a tree in the back-yard which doesn't seem to be doing so well," she says. "I've been sending it some love."

She's been sending my tree love!

I'm on overload because I don't even know what to ask first. Which tree is it? This makes me embarrassed because how could I not know what tree is sick? Although I weirdly don't know that much about trees at all, except that some types really bring on the Here It Comes. Redwoods and Doug firs mostly and why that's true is a whole other topic entirely.

I want to ask her officially, "How do you send a tree love? Is that what you've been doing when you stand there and stare in the alley like that? How do you know they feel the love? Do they send it back?" All of which I kind of know the answer to, but only in my own kind of way. Nothing official. She is talking to me like its Real and Official, which bugs me out. I want to say, "How can you say that to me right here in broad daylight on the street! You don't even know me! What makes you think that I won't write you off right away as a super freak? Sending trees love. What do I look like anyway?" Then somehow I feel like I'm the one who is busted. How could she possibly know?

What *do* I look like anyway?

"Where are you from?" She wants to know. Everyone has to ask.

"I'm from Idaho," I say, and I catch myself before I say more.

I ask her where she's from. Her accent is a weird kind of Sean Connery dialect with a touch of Canada in it.

"Many places. I've moved many times. I've had so many gardens," she says. "This time I planted all my plants in pots so when I have to move on again I can bring them all with me. I'm tired of giving so much and leaving it all behind."

I say, "Sure," because what the hell do you say to that? I don't know where she lives, her yard with plants in pots. I don't know where she's been or what she's given or what all of her different gardens looked like. I ask.

"Well," she says, "there was the desert garden and the English garden and the one in the mountains of Colorado." That's all she says and smiles. Can't really tell if she wants to stay and talk or if she wants to go.

I do and don't want her to tell me more. I do want to say, "What are you doing with your little wheelbarrow and all those plants at night? Where do they come from? Why do you do it?"

I don't want her to say one word about talking to trees, because somehow that's private. That's only between Peter and me, our never-ending silent conversation. And I don't really want to know what makes her think she can just say things like that to me.

I do want to say, "Do you know I'm trying to choose your superhero name?" *ChloroPhyllis.* She smiles. *Queen Plantinum.* Love light everywhere but not giving up a thing. *Lady Green Ray. I'm the Garden Goddess. What's up?*

"Anyway," I say.

"Anyway," she says, "nice to meet you." She turns and walks away, pulling her sunny, yellow love babies.

I want to follow her. I want to be her secret apprentice. I don't want anyone to know. I walk away, pushing the bike, feeling weirdly busted and tingly like she just pulled a giant scab off of me and all I am is pink, raw skin. Talking to trees. I feel it all over. Mrs. Johnson sits on her front porch and waves. I wave back and walk along, wondering how it is that Garden Lady says it like it is. She must know what she wants the world to look like and knows what she has to do to make it that way, rather than looking at the world and assuming that it's just the way it is.

9

JUSTIN WANDERS AROUND HIS room grabbing clothes
and shoving them into a duffle bag for some music festival that
he's going to all weekend that I can't go to because I'm down to
nine dollars and twenty-four cents. God I want to go with him.
A few days in the woods with J-man would really make my day
right about now. My life even.

Justin comes over to where I sit on the corner of his bed and
pushes me back, and we get tangled into a lazy afternoon hang.
I tell him about what happened at the café that I supposedly
work at. I hang around Café Extraction sometimes, just to have
something to do, drink coffee with free refills and watch the
fancy-pants baristas make yoga moms skinny lattes. There's an
inked-up dude that I call Roger the Rocker, the store manager,
who always stands over everyone's shoulder when they're working the espresso maker. He likes to inform people of the right
and not-right way to make coffee and talk crap about the "essen-
tial oil layer" on the top of a perfect cup and how the protein
properties of whole milk make the latte drinking experience
much better.

Today I was standing in line and couldn't take it anymore.
"What the hell are protein properties?" I asked. It wasn't even
my turn.

He never expected anyone to actually ask him. He glared at
me just as he got slammed with a giant drink order and tried to
weasel his way out of answering me straight.

"No. For real. I want to know what protein properties are," I said because I really wanted to know. He sighed like he was bored with me and kept making coffee drinks, but the yoga mom behind me suddenly got interested and asked me what I was talking about. I pointed to Roger the Rocker and said, "Ask him!" because he's the one who says things like that and things like "Crema is gold!" and everyone seems to think he's a god.

Justin laughs and weaves his fingers through mine, high in the air, both of our arms stretched above where we're lying on the bed. Our hands push against each other, and each of us takes turns letting the other hand be the stronger one. My story gets Justin going, and he's on a roll about the history of coffee and the history of coffee snobbery and how it evolved from the grunge era and how it came from Seattle because Seattle never had much to say for itself until Kurt Cobain and Microsoft, which happened to coincide with the coffee movement, and all that fame made them think they knew everything about everything, including coffee, and how all that know-it-all-ness trickled down to Portland ten years later. Or something like that. I never really know what he's talking about.

"I've got an idea," he says, and he rolls half on top of me, a huge smile across his face. "I'm going to make you a T-shirt that says PROTEIN PROPERTIES right across your boobies that you can wear to work!"

Justin is so damn cute. I can't wait to see the look on Roger the Rocker's face the next time I order my coffee.

He lies back down and says he wants to read me something, but he doesn't move to choose a book. We hold hands, stare at his cottage cheese ceiling, and he sighs. "I love being friends with you," he says.

I look at him like he's joking, thinking what's the love part and what's the friends part and why put them together in the same sentence and why bother even saying that at all? The thing is that all of me wants to be next to all of him, so I don't ask, because all of me really *is* next to all of him, love or friends or whatever. I'll take it.

He rolls over on his side, half on me, and slides those fingers down my cheek and they reach into my hair and my ear and chin and I can't breathe. *Love.* I can't breathe. He looks into my eyes, and I breathe way in and he breathes way in too, and that's how we stay for so long.

I want more long. I want to be in his hair, all sun golden, kissy. I want his smooth butter skin. I want honey to drink in the little pool his neck makes where it meets his all-bones collarbone. I want to bite his bottom lip and see if it's full of air or chewy. I want all of him pressing down on me until there's no breath left. I want him to breathe me back into me. I am thinking all of this when he, with those lips and that tongue, finds all these little places and tastes.

"Give me more kisses," he says, "more kisses," which I do. He says, "Not those kisses," with that finger on these lips. "These kisses," and he wraps his warm hands around each breast, his soft face moves slowly across my chest, which melts into his hands. Gives me the shivers. We are so together, not any more him, Justin, and me, Mazzy, that I'm thinking maybe I'll even tell him my real name. Maybe it's time.

We're falling and falling from somewhere high, and I'm loving falling and lying there in the afternoon that is passing slowly, but stops passing all of a sudden when he whispers, "We're friends, right?"

I can't speak because I'm still falling, falling with him, or so I thought, and I'm also trying to decide what to say. *My name's not really Mazzy* had been on the tip of my tongue, about to let so much go. So, what's the right answer? Of course we're friends. The tree outside his room just stands there. He rolls over, looks at me, and first licks and then kisses each eyelid. Nothing so yum has ever touched me like that. He *licks* me.

The warm of his tongue is on the thin of my eyelid and I picture the letters of my real name in my head. J A D E. I crumple them, my name in a tiny ball that I bury somewhere, far away, deep inside, where I shove everything else to forget about it. My fingers twirl in the thick of his hair and I kiss him again, deep and slow, praying while I'm kissing and burying that he'll come searching for my name, all on his own, and dig it up. I pray that it happens soon.

Justin pulls back, pushes the hair from my face, looks at me for a minute, and smiles. "Do you want to stay here while I'm away?" he says. "You can ride my bike."

His bike. I slide my body from under him and sit with my knees to my chest, my arms wrapped around them. "Sure," I say because we're just friends. My voice sounds thin and high. I haven't really known him so long, so what can I say? Besides, *friends* is code for something. Could be *friends* like "buddies only" or friends with "benefits" or the kind of "friends" you are when it's not time to say girlfriend yet. I don't know which it is, and I feel sick. As long as I can swim in those swimmy greens and not have to come up for air, we're friends as far as I'm concerned.

Justin did say he *loves* being friends, which must mean something. And he did ask me to stay at his house and ride his bike, his banana-seat bike with high handlebars. He is such a dork. Such a yummy, eat-me dork. I'll take his room while he's gone for a few days, with I don't know what "friends." And I'll take his bike, too. That has to mean something.

I walk outside to get the bike with his licks and kisses still stinging my face and that all-over everywhere tree *What?* is still standing there. *Whatever. Telling him anything was a dumb idea.* Figure I'll go for a ride to find Garden Lady's house to see all her plants in pots that she can take with her. Begin my secret apprenticeship.

But I change my mind. I don't really feel like it.

10

TONIGHT V-W CAN'T STOP YAKKING. "What are you doing, Maz? Where's Justin, Maz? You gonna wear that purple flowy dress, Maz? Can I, Maz?" She keeps asking questions through my closed door.

"No! I'm wearing it!" I yell. It's not even mine. It's Irina's.

v-w has a nose for when I want to be by myself and she goes digging with it. "Hey, Maz, I was thinking that we should grow some blueberries or strawberries or something. Don't you think that would be cool? Don't you think, Maz?"

She's the reason why the garden has no states now. She's one of those people who thinks it's a good idea to have an idea about something, start it, get a good idea about something else, start that, get a good idea about another thing, and pretty soon they're all tangled and then she's hanging around your bedroom door wanting you to fix things for her.

I want to go to Justin's house. I want to take him up on his offer to stay there for so many reasons, mostly to get away from the witch, but I don't want to go anywhere near the scene of the "we're friends" crime. The punch of that is still stuck in my gut. If we're really "just friends," why would I? I tell myself this. If he goes away again and lets me use his room and we're more than friends, then I can. Tonight, however, I *must* do something else. Luckily, Garden Lady's plants in pots are pulling me out in search of them.

I hop on the banana-seat dork bike and shove the purple

dress under my legs so it doesn't get caught in the wheels. I open myself wide to the rest of the world and ignore everything in me that's trying to convince me to go hang in his room, snuggle in his bed, smell him around me, and look through his stuff in case he wrote something about me and stuck it in the pages of one of his books somewhere.

No.

Tonight I'm Madam Soft Focus with nowhere to go except where I end up, which is a great way to be at night on a bike. You just roll wherever the pull pulls you, and on wheels it all goes much faster and easier. Walking takes too much work. Riding you just flow.

The flow tonight takes me by dark sleeping houses; by one house that's rocking a crazy party I can hear a block away that looks like a high school kegger with tons of kids all over the front yard, two of them puking; by a house with a little ball of light glowing on the side and string lights around a dinner table and quiet little chitchat; by guys playing basketball on the elementary school playground basketball court; by all the plants everywhere so still looking like they're holding their breath, or the others that bother to close at night, which why be one way during the day and another way at night?; by flashes of bar-hopping super freaks crossing the street under the street light—glowing white walking legs and a giant neon afro wig and a bright pink umbrella, even though it's not raining; by streets with parking strips that have no trees in them and other streets that have gigantic trees and also have gigantic houses, which why do only the gigantic houses get gigantic trees?; by the whole world that feels like a wax museum after hours that I'm sneaking around in *until* . . . a house with a yard with plants in pots.

I ditch the bike in an abandoned lot right across the street and crouch down in grass so tall I can hide. It's good cover, but

I keep an eye out for druggie needles and broken glass. The streetlight gives Garden Lady's yard a soft glow. It's not a lawn with all kinds of plants in pots standing around, like I pictured it. Most of the pots are half-buried with only their tops peeking above ground, unless they're hidden by branches or grasses. I only notice them because I know to look for them. There are different size puffs of waving color—a giant reddish tree puff, yellow purple puffs, and lots of shades of green. Some plants are pointy on the end and some grasses are round and floppy. There are flowers and bushes, too. Everything has a place, nestled in to each other. Her parking strip even has plants, piled in, mushed close and creeping around each other's feet. It's a giant plant family, and even though it's all packed in, it is no stateless mess. Everything is watered, fed, and loved. Nothing is duking it out with anything else. No plant feels left out or forgotten. There is enough to go around; everything is taking care of everything else.

Garden Lady's garden makes me want a love-fest yard, and right now my yard is no love fest. I want to go sit right in the middle of her plant party, and I also want to go home. Detangle the continent. It is in serious need. I am trying to decide if it is a good thing to know of a place that makes you want to be a better you or whether it just sucks to realize that you're really not very cool at all. Is anyone camping outside of my house to live on the love-light of my garden?

No.

I wonder how far the love-light of her yard spreads. A few blocks on foot after people walk by. Even more on bike, and more than that by bus when people get bored looking at lots of nothing until their eyes land on her happy plant family. They may not think it, but they see what love actually looks like. They take this with them. What seeds and sun and water and hands and care and time can do. It feeds people, food or no food. I'm trying to figure the distance of the love spread when a feeling hits me square in the chest: spread it even farther! I suddenly see: go plant the continent!

The *yes!* of this idea shoots through my whole body and makes me stand. Just as I do, something moves on her front porch. It's hard to see what because all her plants make the porch private, but something definitely moves. Is Garden Lady watching me watch her plants? Is she wondering what crack head is getting off now? I don't want to scare her, so I crouch back down, but this is ridiculous, too. I'm only going planting. Why hide? So I pretend not to notice if something is noticing me, and I stand back up like it's all good, because it is. I'm just walking out of crack park, un-high, getting on my bike, riding away, and going planting.

I cruise straight home, ditch the bike, squeeze through the stuck gate, and jam my fingers into the dark, moist ground to dig up a few states. Pray that my fingers don't rip a worm in half. I dig around the State of Broccoli, because it's pretty clear what that is, and the State of Bawdy Dill, because it's a flower, too, and can do double duty. The night is watching, I'm sneaking, and I'm weirdly nervous as hell because I feel like I'm going to get caught, which makes me laugh aloud. Caught doing what? Gardening? The no-crime part of this rocks my world.

I hop back on the banana-seat dork bike, haul these little beauties by their tops, and ride down the middle of the street. No one's home at Justin's. I zip right by everyone at Mrs. Johnson's house, and who cares what they think. *Look at me, Peter! I'm doing this, too!* Ride around, buzzed, giggling at what I must look like—a girl with a ponytail in a purple, flowy dress and sweatshirt, riding around the city at night, sitting on a banana seat, one hand high on the handle bar, the other holding a clump of plants with the roots and leaves blowing in the *swoosh* of the breeze. I have no idea where I'll plant them, but then, voila!—a street bench, next to a garbage can, with a dirt patch with nothing in it but dirt presents itself to me. BINGO!

Slide off the banana seat, lean the bike against the back of the bench, and realize I have no shovel. This is really funny. I'm standing here, holding these roots-and-all lovelies, who just want the *ahhhh* of soil so they can go on doing what they do, but I can't dig a hole. There's a stick on the ground, so I lay the plants on the bench careful not to twist or break any leaves, grab the stick, and dig little holes that are just enough. I return the States to their rightful place, hop on my bike, and speed away. I go home, grab the plastic water bottle from the garden, the one I hauled all the way from Skatio that I weirdly still have, and slip into the kitchen. v-w is chanting in her room. I fill the bottle with water, slip back onto my bike, ride to my lovelies, water them all, and ride home again. From what I can tell, no one saw a thing.

I am going to sleep well tonight!

11

V-W DOESN'T EVEN BUG ME ANYMORE. "Where you going, Maz?" she asks as I walk down the hall holding my sleeping bag wrapped in a ball with my notebook and a pen tucked inside. A wild nest of a bun sits high on her head as she stirs a bubbling concoction that smells like dirt and herbs.

"Out," I say. Still giddy from spreading the love last night. I'm feeling bold. Two more nights until Justin's home, so it's a good time to visit his tree and make some planting plans. And other plans too, like maybe getting a job at Café Extraction and figuring how I might be able to hack this living-on-my-own thing and deciding whether or not I should write home and let them know that I'm actually okay. "Have a good night!" I yell as I shut the door. She may not be bugging me that much, but I don't want to stay and chat, either. There's a limit to everything.

Mrs. Johnson wants to know where I'm going, too. "Just visiting a friend," I yell. She's the only one in her yard tonight.

"All right then," she says, and she leans against a post on her porch, her eyes on my back as I walk down the block.

Lights are on in Justin's house. His roommates are home, but he said I could stay, so I walk into his backyard and find a spot so that the tree is between the house and me. A little privacy would be nice. The sleeping bag opens with a quick unzip. I shimmy in and settle with my spine against the trunk. My favorite way to be. Branches start two-stories high on the long stretch of trunk and reach outward beyond the chain-link fence, like they're trying to touch the neighbor's house. Far-off sounds drift into the yard—a plane, a truck, traffic, a band practicing. The tinny sound of a cymbal, muffled guitar, and the constant repeat of the same verse float across the neighborhood. There are so many night routines in one city block. TV-watching, car-fixing, dinner-making, bath-taking, daydreaming, fighting. All this and yet the night also feels so still. And then there's me, snuggled with this tree, which feels so lonely in this little square yard. I wish that it knew its family.

I wiggle around to get on my knees, still in the sleeping bag, like a caterpillar in a cocoon, place my hands on the thick of the knotty bark, and slide the tips of my fingers into crevices. Sometimes when I do this with Peter it can feel like all of me drains into him and I can feel in my body how things move inside his trunk, the up and also down of his flow and the deep quiet. If there is a place where forever lives, that's it. The quiet can be so deep and wide you can't feel the sides of it, like floating. You have to let yourself go. The more you let go, the more you can know, but there is so much space between the truths that a tree knows that it can take some time before you know what's what. The trick is to not get caught up with worry about when the feeling will hit you, which can make you miss it altogether.

Kneeling in the night stillness of Justin's yard with my hands on the tree, memories of Peter start flooding in. The first time I saw him in the Family Circle by my house. He was growing over the stump of a burned-out old tree. You almost couldn't see the charred stump with Peter's roots stretching over it. It even looked like maybe there weren't two trees at all, but one fire cave at the base of an old trunk and extra roots growing from a few feet off the ground. But it was two trees. One gone and Peter living right on top, like there was too much wide-open, gone trunk stump that needed to be covered. It always made me think of closing people's eyes for them when they die.

I wrote Peter letters. I don't even know why except that it was kind of like a message in a bottle that someone, somewhere, somehow maybe might answer. I didn't really believe I'd get an answer, but I secretly hoped that one would come. I don't know how many letters I wrote, but I put them all in a tin, dug a hole in the center of the Family Circle, and kept them buried there for safekeeping.

The first time I ever got an answer back was days after I'd left a letter for him. My heart was broken from looking at so many stubby hillsides with barely any trees left. *I sleep in a wood bed.* I wrote. *I wipe my butt with toilet paper. Lily uses crayons. Why do you have to go away so we can have these things?* I never expected an answer, but the next time I was lying in the fire cave, resting there, a quiet thought came into my head. Three of them, actually. *Using us is not the problem* popped in first. *Nothing works if there's only taking* came next. Then *Live in what will outlive you.* With the words came an easy peace that spread throughout my body. I didn't believe that Peter was actually *talking* to me. It was more like there was a whole world of things I could learn lying inside that Family Circle. I felt part of something way bigger than me that anyone could be a part of if they just lay there and got quiet enough and listened.

The feeling stayed with me, but with each passing day it left, little by little, until there were only words that had no feeling attached to them at all. The words without the deep-peace feeling is what haunted me. *Nothing works if there is only taking* was pretty clear. But *Live in what will outlive you.* What did that mean? Redwood trees will outlive me. What am I supposed to do? Be a hermit and live inside a tree? Living in a town like Skatio doesn't exactly offer help deciphering what trees have to say.

The sudden clang of a pan in the kitchen sink of Justin's house makes me nearly jump out of my skin. Cool night air sneaks into the sleeping bag, and I shrug the puffy down tighter around my neck, lie down, and curl into myself, cozy, picturing Justin's whacky roommate setting the table before going to bed, arranging her little glass animal figures at the top of each fork.

I shove my sleeping bag into a bunch so there's a mini pillow under my head and breathe in the musty, sappy smell of Justin's tree. Stuff from my folks' house pops into my head now, too. Tree ears by the kitchen sink and by Mom's makeup mirror—those weird fungi that grow on trees like little shelves. Dad breaks them off and writes notes to Mom and leaves them around the house for her. *Luv U Birdie* he wrote on one. He calls her Birdie. My mom's latch-hook rugs, the huge one on the living room wall with two owls on a branch. The small one in the kitchen that reads, *Love Thy Neighbor. Just don't get caught!* Mom was so into her rugs for a while that Dad said she was going to wake up one day all covered in yarn. "My latch-hook wife," he said, and he pulled the hair away from the back of her neck and kissed her there. Lily and I ran away pretending she was a yarny monster, because who really wants to see your parents making out?

Everything Lily. Her weird little piles of stuff she would collect. "This is to take care of Sugar!" she said about a pile that included a wooden spoon, plastic bowl, magazine, and a candle she stole from Mom's bathroom. "Who's Sugar?" I asked. "My horse!" she said like it was obvious, holding a broom.

My dad's yellow lunch pail by the coffee maker he always packs with four sandwiches and a stack of cookies. The sound of the truck that loggers call the *crummy* that picks him up way too early to haul him off into the woods for work. His spiky shoes he leaves outside the front door—his corks. A weird name for work shoes. His worn-out La-Z-Boy recliner where he crashes after his shift and complains about how hard his life is. Mom doesn't let him get away with the complaining.

"Oh, you love it, Stanley Reynolds, and I don't want to hear anymore about it," she called out from the kitchen, yelling over the sound of whatever she was frying for dinner one late afternoon. Dad looked at me and Lily, sitting on the couch, watching TV, and rolled his eyes like, *Here we go again*, because once Mom gets going she doesn't stop. Especially since Gramps's accident. "You and your brother and your father would not get up at 4:00 a.m. to climb those godforsaken trees, that could kill you, I might add, if you didn't love it. Or spend six days a week in those soggy forests if you didn't love being there. Every single day you go out in those woods you put the welfare of this entire family in jeopardy. Do you realize that? Because of some tree that could fall on you because of some stupid thing that someone wasn't even paying attention to. You do not do that unless you love what you do, Stanley. So quit complaining." She never bothered to come out of the kitchen. By the end of her rant Dad was snoring, or at least pretending to.

He doesn't even take a rest on Saturday mornings. He wakes so early, like he does all week, and I hear him at 4:00 a.m. Sometimes the job he's working doesn't take all the trees they fall that week. There's always a little bit left, a few leaners or busted snags. He goes and cuts what's left to sell for firewood. Make a little extra money. Sometimes I go with him. We pack butter and rolls for breakfast and I cozy next to him in the truck, staring out the window at the cold, gray fog on the way to the site.

Dad was climbing up and down the hill one Saturday, slipping and sliding with his chainsaw, but catching himself always from falling. Jumping over stumps and logs, cutting what's left. It's true. He loves it out there. You can tell because he's singing, some old song he's half making up as he goes. I'm sitting warm in the cab, watching him take his saw to torn-apart, nothing-left pieces of tree, the clear-cut so big, looking bombed, when a feeling comes over me: those logs aren't just tree trunks that fell. That pile stacked next to him is a pile of bodies. What was alive. I *know* this is true, but I would never dream of saying anything. It's just not something you say, especially not to Mr. King-of-the-Woods. Mr. You-Can-Buy-Me–a-Case-of-Beer-Already-Because-You-Know-I'll-Climb-That-Tree-Faster-Than-You. It's just not something you say.

But for some reason that Saturday morning I can't help myself. I roll down the window and start yelling, "Why do you keep taking more?" This knowing is in all of me that those trunks are not only something that was alive but also what makes everything else alive. Air I breathe. What I dream. I want to yell DON'T YOU *KNOW YOU'RE CUTTING MY DREAMS!*

His chainsaw is loud and he doesn't even notice me at first, but then he does. He flips off the saw, standing down the hill in his dirty Carhartts. "What's wrong, kiddo?" he yells to me. His dumb suspenders, shirt with cut-off sleeves, doing what everyone around there does. "What are you going on about?" he yells.

I shove the truck door open, get out like I'm going to go somewhere, but there's nowhere to go, so I stand there crying because he doesn't even know what he's doing. Crying because *Nothing works if there is only taking* and he thinks everything still all works. But it doesn't, and how do I know that? He drops his chainsaw and his smile goes pretty quick. He comes running straight for me with his *I'm going to set you straight* stare. He's running up and over downed trees like they're toothpicks until he's right in front of me, his hands on my shoulders, fingers digging in deep. "What is your problem now?" The mad in him running at me, morning coffee on his breath. "It's only firewood," he barks, like it's obvious. But it wasn't. It's not. I'm looking out over nothing left, trying to figure how can he know the woods as well as he does and not *know* that?

"Lord love a duck," he says, and he loosens his grip and shakes me by the shoulders, but not too hard. "Don't be a tree hugger, kiddo. Whatever you do, *do not be a tree hugger.*" He smacks me on the back and goes back down the hill to keep chopping logs, but not before he turns and gives me one last *I'm serious now* stare because it was only Saturday after all and it really was only a stack of firewood.

What was I going to say?

Is anyone doing the math?

The woodsy smell of Justin's tree fills my nose and my lungs. There's so much I don't know, and I breathe it out of me as if I can give it away. And then I breathe the tree back in. I breathe out the very long list of everything I have no idea what to do about—Justin, v-w, one dollar and twenty-eight cents left, fleas, little Lily, that kid, Nelson. There's so much more that could make it a very long list, and I run out of breath. I breathe the tree back in. I do this over and over, and with everything I breath out, I shove new thoughts in: *What should I plant and where? What should this tree be named?* Goliath is the name that comes to me, but it's a dude name and this tree feels like a girl. It needs to be something rad, like Angelina Jolie.

Then it comes to me: *Your name is Joliath.*

Justin is home a day early. "Mazzy! Mazzy! MAZZZYYY!" he yells the next morning, twirling around the backyard with his arms outstretched, head thrown back, face to the sky.

I sit in the sleeping bag and rub at my face, trying to understand what the hell is going on.

Justin kneels in front of me, happy. His cold hands grab mine. "I just got turned on to the best hip-hop-space-alien music ever!" His eyes are wide and so bright green. "And I met these crazy tree-climbing dudes. You'd love them! And there's some tree-camp thing and you should come!"

My brain is not computing because he's not supposed to be home until tomorrow. "How did you know I was here?" I pull my hands from his and back into the sleeping bag because we're "just friends," so I cannot give him any signs.

He's doesn't get the point and sits down close next to me. "My roommates told me that you fell asleep here last night," he says, but as soon as he sits down he stands again. "Are you hungry? Because I am starving. Wait right here." He runs, all limbs, to the back door. "I'll make us some breakfast," he calls as he disappears inside.

This was not supposed to happen. Now Justin doesn't even know that I specifically did not take him up on his offer to stay in his room and it looks like I am all in his life. Like I couldn't be away from his stuff. Like I want him or something, which is true, but he's not supposed to know that.

His being home could seriously mess with my secret mission.

My deal to me: above all else go ahead with the plan for tonight.

Remind me, Joliath! Remind me!

12

OH MY GOD. I'M SUCH AN IDIOT. Such a freaking idiot.
Curled in a ball with covers pulled over my head, holding them
in a knot close to my chest. I can't stop shaking.

Around midnight I was walking down the street pulling the
neighbor's wagon that I borrowed and filled with pieces of the
continent for planting, when I heard a voice. "Where you going
with all those plants?" Scared the daylights out of me. I turned
and looked into the dark front porch where Mrs. Johnson's voice
came from, but I couldn't see a soul. "I asked you, sugar, where
are you going tonight?" I was busted already and hadn't even
gotten very far. Never thought to have an excuse ready, so I stood
there with a dopey, guilty smile plastered on my face. "You going
to that young man's house?" she asked.

"Yeah," I tell her. "I'm going to Justin's."

"Uh-huh," she says like she doesn't believe me or doesn't
approve, I don't know which. "I'm keeping an eye on him, sweet-
heart. Let me just say this: you take care of your heart, you hear?"

I smile my dopey, busted smile. "I will," I say, even though
now my heart hurts.

Oh my God. I'm such a mess. Dried blood on my fingers. I
can't even swallow.

I pretend to go to Justin's and sneak through his yard and
his neighbors yard to get to the next street. A hole in the ground
makes me trip, which knocks the wagon over and makes every
dog in the neighborhood have a hissy. Find my feet, lay the plants

back in the wagon, and navigate the darkness in between the spill of streetlights. Whatever about Justin. I'm getting all Garden Goddess love fest now, plotting how I'm going to change the world, or at least three feet of it.

The burned-up house is all dead house, no life anywhere. Soot still darkens the entire front, strips of siding hang like tape that's lost its stick, windows are sockets with no eyes looking out anymore. But the night is going to be all right because I'm bringing life back to no life. Try to decide where the plants should land because the State of Chives needs to get into the ground before all that punk-rock purple flower loses its freak. I dig into the soil that is bone dry and mixed with chunks of charred wood and is desperate to mix with roots. The green of the plants is crazy electric next to the burnt earth. It is clear to me: plants are life. Green is gold. *The world needs more green gold!* I dig and wonder if anyone is watching.

The *dom dom dom* of the car bass is far off at first. I feel it in my chest, but I don't think much of it until it's loud, like right-near-me loud, and I can even hear the music more than the bass. The house is on an alley and I am kind of on the front, but mostly on the side of the house so I won't be seen. Where no one can see me.

In the alley it's the NO MERCY stupid yellow freak-trap on wheels. Two dudes get out, and I know. Skeleton-bone sweatshirts zipped over their faces and heads so there is no one to look at. Only a hood of bones. Dark ghosts are heading right for me and I don't even move. *What could possibly happen?* I think. *I'm gardening!*

Oh god. What I didn't know.

All at once it's face jammed, dirt face. Who cares about the shovel cutting my face. All chives all pieces all dirt all everywhere. NO MERCY sits on me and digs through my clothes, my pockets, my bag. "THIS IS MY HOUSE, YO!" Eating dirt. "WHAT ARE YOU DOING HERE?" Getting into all my stuff to see who freaking knows what. Neck is killing me. "MY HOUSE! YOU HEAR?" Squished down. I'm eating worms, must be, because everything tastes metal, tastes rotten, the edge of the shovel pressed into my flesh. Until he's up and I'm down. "DO YOU HEAR ME?" and some hand on my head and I am not allowed to look at him, but that shovel slides across my face and I am sure this is it. I am sure of it. Until ghost feet leave and NO MERCY car trap *dom dom dom* stays in my chest forever until I don't feel it anymore.

There are eyes inside the house next door. Watching everything. Doing nothing.

I don't make a move, for however long it takes, and then run all the way home, not looking back.

The stupid flip clock on the junk desk reads 7:45 when I wake. Hurt inside and out. Blood mud mess. Cheek cut. Call me scar face. Call me idiot. Call me what was I thinking? What am I ever, ever thinking? I didn't even try to yell.

The soft of the bed holds me where I lie curled in a ball, looking at all the crap in this room that isn't mine. My stupid girly backpack, the only thing from before. Wooden fruit crates stacked on top of each other to serve as a makeshift dresser. And there, in the way back of the bottom crate, a black furry head sits amidst the clothes, peering at me.

Tater got in.

"C'mon," I say. "Come here." The fleabag booger *thump-thump drags* his rotten self over to my bed and curls next to me, and this time I let him. "You win," I say. Lying all fleabag flopped out, trying to figure if it is beauty or a curse that Tater got into my room. I don't know. Maybe beauty, because he's purring and what else is there really besides warm, cozy kitty purring?

A knock on the door breaks the quiet, and J-man busts in, singing, still flying from some other planet. He takes one look at me and stops, his mouth and eyes open wide. "What happened to you?"

I don't want it to, but it feels so good to see him. "Nothing, really," I say. "I fell off the bike."

"My poor Mazzy!" he says, and he comes over to the bed and kisses me all over. I hurt too much to make him stop.

"My cheek will make it," I tell him when I can't smile.

"I know, I know," he says, kissing where it isn't cut. "They always do." He crawls in with me and Tater and it's true: this is the only thing I want. Just quiet. Just warm. Just purring. Just kisses. Just Justin.

We lie for a long time and I know because I am holding my breath because if I don't, it's all over. But Justin has to go and talk. "My sweet, sweet Mazzy, tell me everything," he says, and that's it. It's all falls, waterfalls. Tears and snot. Nothing that I can hold back. I can't even talk for crying, and even if I could, what would I say? That Tater finally got in? That why can't he be my home? That everything growing is more home to me than anything else? That the world needs more green gold before it's too late? That everything growing always gets whacked?

Justin watches me have no words. He wipes tears, he kisses, he leans over to the window next to my bed and breathes on it over and over until it's moist. He takes his finger and writes, WHENEVER YOU'RE READY in what's left of his wet breath. He knows I didn't fall off the bike.

"So, my goddess," he sits up. "The decision is made. We leave tonight for the camp-tree thing I was telling you about. You are not staying here alone. You are coming with me." He hops off the bed, grabs my backpack, and starts packing. "It might be chilly. We need to keep you warm." He stuffs my bag with clothes that are not mine and my notebook, which I never let anyone touch. "I've got some warm clothes you can use."

"Okay," I say because he's where I want to be anyway. Maybe I should say no, but I really don't know. I really don't know anything.

13

THE CHEMICAL BURN OF AMMONIA worms its way through my head and jolts me awake. Smelling salts. Not snapped and held under my nose, but broken and shoved up, like my nostrils are stuffed with Tootsie Rolls. I unstuff each side, but the stench still sears my sinuses. Silver-green, shaggy branches blot out the sun overhead and erase any hint that the sky is blue. I look around and try to figure what's what when I'm suddenly seized by two facts: the fact that I blacked out and the reason why I did.

I'm Here. And when I say, "Here," I do not mean some-flipping-where up North. *Justin got it wrong! Way, way wrong.*

We piled into the van late last night because some dude had to work late so we couldn't leave earlier. It was a cargo van with no seats or windows. Bunches of scratchy flannel moving blankets were spread across the floor. I curled into Justin, who was all love-light, so soft and tender, holding me to bring me back from where I'd been. He was mine for hours, driving in the dark, with three other dudes and a mannequin—which is a whole other story—piles of ropes and climbing gear. I didn't pay attention to a single thing because he told me we were going north, so I didn't care where because I was with him and he was the only place I wanted to be.

Now. HERE. I. AM.

At six a.m. or some way-too-early time we were all unpacking the van. I kind of help because I'm so sore from NO MERCY.

I'm looking around this campground thinking *I didn't know there were redwoods in Washington. These are some rocking redwoods. Oh, redwoods. It's been so long. You smell so good. You smell like home.* Then I think, *This looks a lot like home.* So I ask, "What park are we in?" Curious, because it seems weird that there are so many redwoods in Washington, but my gut is telling me we are not in Washington. Nowhere close.

Here It Comes times ten. Times a hundred.

"Humboldt State Park," someone says.

"Humboldt, California?" I say, and I do this weird laugh thing that I can't stop that has tears mixed in, and I can't breathe. Justin wants to know what's got me freaked, and I tell him, "This is hilarious!" My body all sore, my face cracked, heaving. Justin wants to know why I'm crying. "I'm laughing, dude! I'm laughing!" I tell him. "You have no idea! I'm laughing!" I say, and I force a laugh, yelling in my head, *I RAN AWAY FROM HERE, DUDE! I RAN AWAY AND THEY ARE LOOKING FOR ME!*

I can't breathe. I'm sucking in air, and next thing I know someone thought it was a good idea to shove these things up my nose. You're only meant to break them, but whatever. They were stuck in my nose and now all I smell is ratty electric chemical cat piss.

Skatio is two towns away.

Here It Comes times a million. Welcome home, Jade.

14

THIS MUCH I KNOW: I'm breathing. That's a start. I'm breathing more than freaking, which only means that freaking made me tired and I had no choice but to settle down. I'm breathing and I'm watching.

Justin was all, "Mazzy, baby, chill," and I was dizzy like I wanted the lights out. He brought me over to a log on the ground. "Sit," he said, and I did. I kept smiling hard and held back the tears. He wanted to know, "You freaking because of yesterday?" I smiled and nodded. "That must have been heavy," he said. Smile. Nod. NO MERCY. That's not even half of it. "Just look at the trees, baby; they'll calm you down," he said, which pushed me right over the edge.

"These trees will *not* calm me down!" I yelled in his face, which I yelled instead of, "How do you not know which way is *south*?"

He got quiet and put up the tent, all the while thinking, *This girl is nuts.* I'm sure. When he was done, he called to me, "Chill in here, Maz, until I'm done helping unloading everything." And then he left me alone to go lend a hand.

Sounds of people talking drifted in to where I sat inside the stuffy musty tent, breathing, peering at the scene through the tiny square screen, not making any sense of how it is that I'm actually back home. But stuck in a tent didn't help a thing, and I moved back out to the log, where at least I could get a better lay of the land. I needed to find my feet and my butt, both of which

86

are under me right now. This much I know. That and the fact that I've got dream face in my cheeks and jaw—numb, prickly, and tingly, like when your limbs fall asleep.

All I'm good for now is seeing what's right in front of me: at six o'clock is me sitting in front of our tent on a log. Nine o'clock is a little walk to a river, probably the Eel River, *Which means that you're pretty close, Peter.* There's a long cement rectangular picnic area filled with supplies like food, pots and pans, water bottles, a hunting bow, and ropes. Lucky that the picnic area is covered, because everywhere else is very moist. There's a fire pit. Nine to twelve o'clock is four more little tents, and three o'clock is a dirt road that runs from the park into our campsite and around the inside of this circle. Growing green things sprout tall in the center of it all.

The Here It Comes is not whispering now. It's not even yelling. It's just all there is. My whole body is wide-awake, worried, wondering. There are people unpacking, talking, hanging. A few guys are goofing off, saying, "Duuuude" a lot, wrestling and calling each other "girly man" in fake-German Arnold Schwarzenegger accents. They're like puppies. Groovy hippie chicks waltz around, one whose butt crack is a non-stop show. Two dudes have dreads, and so far no one seems to have recently had theirs chopped off.

This is not some tree-camp thing. It's a supply run for a tree sit—hippies living in the trees so no one cuts them down. Living here for as long as it takes to get the logging company to stop cutting or they get arrested, whichever comes first. Some folks are going to stay here at base camp collecting supplies, and some are going to run all this stuff to where the rest are living in the treetops. There are upwards of twenty-five trees tied together and I don't know how many kids living there. Justin met one of these dudes at the music festival he went to and thought it would be rad to see what it's like.

Peter, are you getting all of this?

This is one of those pop-up camps that everyone at The What Not is making plans to wipe out. "Those no-good, dirty, tree-hugging hippies." They are sitting around, probably right now, not working because of these hippies in these trees. Stopping them from working means they don't get paid, which makes them very, very mad. "All for some *freaking trees*." And here I am with Them.

If Liza saw me with these kids she would be speechless. And that never happens.

Justin is going on and on about everything and nothing. Some trip about activism that he goes on because butt-crack blondie wants to know, "Are you an activist?"

He's on a roll. "I'm *not* an activist," he says, "because activism is the division of labor related to social change." I cannot believe him. "It is a specialized job, just like any other specialized job, meant to create social and or environmental change." He makes it all sound so ho-hum, like he's talking about the weather. I don't even know if I'm getting it right, what he says. "So if people think other people are activists, they don't have to do anything because they think someone else is already taking care of it."

How he can talk like that but not know enough to tell me where, exactly, we were going is way beyond me. Then again, I didn't even ask. "Some tree-camp thing," he said.

Justin balances on a rock, yakking, looking good enough to eat. Screw him. "Ninety-nine percent of what is called activism today is something that will make no difference to history," he keeps going on. Does he even know who he's talking to? These thoughts I'm sure make him come right over and stand in front of me. He puts his hands out, ready to go. "C'mon, Maz. You feeling better now? Let's go somewhere!" He thinks the whole world is for playing. "What do you want to do? Climb trees?

Hike? Help build pods?" He sees butt-crack blondie and uses his hand to wave to her.

This is not some nighttime game of who planted carrots next to the bus stop. How can he not know? "No, no. I'm cool for now," I say instead of, "You want to know how for-real this place is? This place is called the *trenches* by folks in town." But I have to bite my lip because there's too much yesterday and today mushing together. It's just not the time for me, in front of everyone, to tell him about how all those loggers want to eat these kids for breakfast—these *smelly, freaky people who just make a lot of fuss, but really do no goddamn good except giving me something to take aim at* is what Nelson likes to say.

This is so not funny. "This story does not have a happy ending," I say.

"What are you talking about?" Justin asks, and his eyes are not even on me but looking all around the whole camp, thinking, *This girl is nuts.* I tell him forget it. I'm a mess from getting whacked. "Yeah, chill," he says, and in front of everyone he gives me a long hug that quiets everything down. "Mazzy, baby," he whispers. He said *baby* again, and that makes three times. "These woods will bring you back. I promise."

What he doesn't know.

15

CAMP COOKING SOUNDS BREAK THE silence of the sleeping forest, tiny little sounds that barely make a dent in these old, wet woods. Nestled into the puff of sleeping bags and the warm neck of J-boy, which is the only thing that finally quieted my body into rest last night. With an ear open for any footsteps that might be mean, sleep didn't come easy. But warm is good. Sleep is good. Even a little resets your brain.

Justin snoozes as I pull my limbs from our tangle and feel around the floor for my notebook and backpack, which are shoved into a corner. The sound of the tent zipper cuts through the air. The small opening is enough to crawl through and a camp chair by the opening is the perfect place to take it all in. Silent trees loom. For all their massive size, they make so little noise. It's the quiet itself that's loud—it fills the space and wants more, pushes into my ears and puffs up like a sponge, not at all disturbed by teeny-weeny us, someone making a meal.

The canvas cradle of the chair holds the lump of me and a mellow screw-it feeling permeates my entire body. Life was going one way and all of sudden it's going somewhere else. Somewhere home. Hard to sort out. The good part is that being here is turning into more of a slowly-sinking-in shock, instead of a freak-shock. A weird mosh of NO MERCY and Justin and now in these woods that I used to play in, *where I learned to talk to you, Peter*, where so much has gone down, where it's home and not home all at the same time. *Now what?*

It was just plain dumb to plant someone's house. There are so many on-the-street places that need green, but no. I had to pick some burned-out hell house when my planting-at-night plans were just shaping up—living in the love-light of the Garden Lady, being her secret apprentice, planting in the places where there are no plants. It made so much sense. I was redeeming myself. It was my own deal that didn't have to be seen by anyone, and I wouldn't have to choose sides. Planting could take place in the dark and green would still grow and that was good enough for me.

One by one, people emerge from the colorful bubbles of their tents. They stand bleary-eyed and stretch in the cool morning air. The day is gentle and less scary and maybe it's even going to be okay. The truth is, home is still at least eight miles away, so I'm not *that* close. And I'm in a state park. Anyone who lives here doesn't really go to state parks. My family doesn't. We just know trails we like and places Dad likes to hunt. So it's not like anyone will find me. Besides, the tree-sitting hippies are not causing any trouble here. They're only hanging out. And stockpiling supplies, but no one would really *know* that.

I tell myself these things.

My deal with me is to hold my breath and go with it—all of it—until the van goes back in a day or two. Try to be normal, stay out of the way, write in my notebook, and see what happens.

No sooner do I write, *I'm just going to go with all of it,* then I look from my notebook up at the trees, and how can you ignore these trees? ALL OF IT written like big bold letters in my head. I shove my notebook into my backpack and set off for a hike.

Light green that is almost yellow, and dark shades that turn almost gray, mix with streams of sunlight that sneak in between the jagged, needley branches trying to reach the forest floor. Forget the sky. Chunky, spongy red-brown trunks reach up for as far as the eye can see and extend from side to side way more than I can reach around.

The woods look so un-scary now. Not like when I left.

The trail runs right next to the riverbed, and the wide brown green flow moves along next to me. It is the Eel. The river brings back so many memories. Early morning days off fishing with Dad, because he didn't have a son to teach those things to. His weird way, his too rough, fingers double thick. The muscles rippled in his arm just under his skin at his elbow when he reeled something in. "Come here, kiddo!" He'd be excited. "Come take this monster off the hook!" The smelly fish slime was gross, but I got good at it.

We'd go to the Hermit Tree sometimes after fishing and poke around the home that was built inside the burned-out redwood. A hermit lived there years ago and managed to build three floors. The floors were gone, but you could see the door and the window and the table he built. People say he even had a wood stove in there.

After fishing we'd hang at The What Not, where everyone would drink beer, complain, and do weird drag races. They backed their trucks to each other, chained the back bumpers together, and jammed on the gas pedal to see which guy could drag the other guy out of town first. I watched and wandered around the giant tree trunks carved into the shape of Bigfoot, set there for some dumb tourist to buy.

The hiking path veers away from the Eel, heads deeper into the woods, and the sweet smell of moist living and dying fills my nose. Limbs and branches and fallen-down trees are rotting and growing things all at the same time. It's not one or the other, but both. Ancient wood worlds stand on either side of the path, each one hundreds to a thousand years old, a whole planet unto itself. I'm just some annoying mosquito buzzing in this so-old earthy outer space.

How is it that these woods are the deepest peace and cause so much trouble at the same time? Endless arguing at home. Early morning whisper fights between Mom and Dad that used to wake me up, especially after some logging buddy lost an arm or died. That happened more than once. And it got worse after Gramps's leg. People in town got weird when Gramps got hurt. They stayed away. Mom said they were convinced the bad luck would rub off on them, but Dad thought she was just making nonsense. Gramps wasn't even living with us, but I think she was right and they stayed away from us, too, because we're related. Mom was spooked and didn't want Dad to work. Not anymore.

One morning she refused to make his lunch. The *crummy* sat outside, the truck with Dad's logging buddies waiting in the early morning dark. He stomped around making his own lunch. Mom warned him, "Don't open that door!" Their fuss reached to where I lay in bed listening, thinking that when the fight got quiet he'd say, once and for all, "Okay. I won't go back," and we'd go fishing instead.

But he didn't say that. "I'd rather die with my boots on!" is what he said, not bothering to whisper as he left the house.

"Dead's not even what I'm worried about!" Mom whisper-yelled before he slammed the door.

Dad runs his own show and we never have good health insurance, so Mom is less worried about his dying and more worried about what she'd do if he got seriously hurt. Seems like dead is easier to think about than a hurt Dad and a hurt husband and no health insurance and no paycheck and a mountain of bills and no help and two kids and, and, and.

"You gotta stop making two plus two equal twenty, Birdie," is what Dad said when he came home and wasn't so mad.

"Yeah, but two ten times is." She stood in the doorway to the kitchen, taking a minute from making dinner before her night shift. "You're just not putting it all together." She threw a couch pillow at where he was lying in his recliner, and a mad smile spread across her face, like she knew there wasn't a single thing she could do to keep him from his work. And she was right.

Wandering around these woods that are like home, forest bliss starts to set in. With each passing tree I start to really feel them. I should head back to camp so Justin doesn't worry, but the call of the trees is louder. It's like they want me to spend time, really *be* with them.

Ahead on the path is an odd and funny tree. Three huge redwoods are merged together at the base into what looks like one trunk that's about three elephants wide. In the middle is a hole, like the three trees are standing around where a fourth used to be. They each reach in different directions, and the top of the fourth tree has worked its way into the others higher up, still living somehow, even though it's not attached to the ground.

The pull of this tree is strong. It invites me in, and there really is an inside to go into. Part of me wants to keep on walking, get back to camp, but ALL OF IT is on repeat in my head. I sit on a rotten stump to get my courage either way—ignore the tree that's calling to me or be late to camp.

Sitting in the middle of a thousand wood years is terrifying, sure to bring on the Here It Comes. I don't want to see. Not right now.

But what's really going to happen anyway? It's just a dumb tree. ALL OF IT.

I duck down through an opening and crawl through the hole until I'm encircled by sweet-smelling red-brown wood that is soft and smooth and black from fire in spots. So far, so good. It's dark and close and stretches far above my head, but there is enough room. A deep breath in and this tree invites me in more. There is room to climb, but I'm fine where I am, looking out at what looks at this tree. It's cool like a basement and tight around my head. The everywhere damp eats every sound. There is no echo. And then it happens: my fingers tingle and my heart goes heavy like a stone, only it's not heavy and it's not a stone. It's just this incredible pull down. Here It Comes. My heart seems to go away or blend into everything else. This earthy, dream soup. I'm swimming in it.

I asked for it, I know, but I'm suddenly not so sure, and panic begins to rise. I force myself to breathe and let the deep, slow quiet run through all of me until ease settles my mind and my heart feels roots. It's true, inside a thousand wood years *is* a very good place. But the What Abouts start to kick in: What about Justin? What about that kid? And Nelson? What about *that*? What about Dad and Mom and Lily? What about being right smack in the middle of everything I tried to get away from?

What comes from this kind, always-here tree is *What about nothing*. This feels like a hug that's meant to make me feel better, a remedy for The What Abouts that are way bigger than three elephants wide and as high as the sky. My body keeps doing the seven hundred million things that it does: flow blood, move muscles, breathe in air that's made right here, right now by this tree around me, in the middle of everything I tried to leave. A big, tree breath in fills my lungs, deeper this time, and a sweet peace spreads through me now, filling my heart like the flame in a hot air balloon.

16

HANGING OUTSIDE THE TENT watching everyone do their thing, it's clear that I wasn't totally right: there aren't only guys who say *duuuude* and girls with their pants falling down. There are all kinds of people. Most are longer-haired, some have dreads, lots have piercings and tattoos, and many girls don't wear a bra. People come and go all the time, helping, it seems. The guys who were wrestling like Arnie puppies left at the end of the day yesterday. They were climbing rats, either rock climbers or tree climbers, who thought it would be cool to hang in the trees for a while and share their climbing know-how. There is still no sign of a guy with chopped-off dreads, and I am not about to be the one to ask about it.

On my hike back yesterday, after being with the tree, I chose its name: Jedediah, after the Jedediah Smith State Park. The park is named after some guy. So it's a tree named after a park named after a guy. I just like to say it. JED-E-DI-AH.

Justin made a beeline when he saw me return and said that I needed to play it cool because after my first-day freak and then disappearing for most of the day everyone was beginning to wonder if I was a little sketchy. "They're not so sure about you," he said, which made me laugh for so many reasons.

I was thinking, *I'm not sure about me either, so why should they be?* I'm the closest they've probably come to having The Enemy camp with them—daughter of a logger and all. What would they say or do if they knew? I may be sketchy, but not in the ways they're worried about. After all, I heart trees more than anyone. And what are they worried about anyway? It looks like we're only people camping, so why is everyone acting so weird and secret? In a day or two *some* of these kids will be in a tree owned by a lumber company that doesn't let anyone on their land, which means they're *about to be* illegal. But for now, why, especially around me, are certain things whispered about or why is the conversation taken somewhere else? Who's sketch then?

I was laughing, thinking all of these things, but I stopped laughing because Justin stood there looking at me. "Where have you been, anyway? You've been gone for hours," he said. He seemed kind of mad, but he actually looked more worried. "You're acting really flipping weird. I don't know what happened to you back in Portland, but I wish you would either tell me what's up or get a grip."

Honest-to-goodness concern bled through his voice, reminding me that he didn't know a single thing about what was going on. I hadn't told him anything. The soft green of eyes was wide open, inviting me in, and no one had ever looked at me like that before. I wanted to go in.

"I just went for a walk," I said. "I needed some time with the trees."

"Yeah, well, we had no idea where you were." He turned and started to walk away to help with dinner, but turned back around. "I hope you found Mazzy in those woods. I'd like to hang with her again."

Jade, I thought, and I smiled. "Yeah." I said. "Okay."

Justin waited for a minute, like he didn't want to walk away. "Will she be coming to dinner this evening?" His swimmy greens looked like he might like me again.

"Yes." I said. "She will."

"Good." He took a quick bow like some butler. "Please tell the young lady that I will be expecting her."

Everyone's been acting nice today and let me be. Justin must have told them that I got whacked back in Portland, and they're giving me room, which is a very good thing. The deep tree quiet has stayed in my heart and in my bones throughout the day, settling my nerves, and all my worlds are nowhere except here, on this ground that I know so well.

Butt-crack blondie shows up with a cup of tea, which she didn't have to do. A pack of blond dreads hangs down her back, her jeans are too big, and layers of shirts are bulky on her body. "I'm Woodruff," she says and hands me the cup as she sits on the ground next to where I sit cross-legged outside our tent. "You doing okay?" Checking me out for herself. Big, blue eyes are bright in her freckly face. Queen of the Camp. Running the show. She's funny because she talks sweet and laughs a little after she speaks, which makes you think she's nervous, but then she tells you how things are and then you know that she's in charge.

"I'll be cool," I tell her. The scent of chai wafts from my cup. "No worries." For the first time in days I actually mean it.

"Cool," she says, and she draws pictures with her finger in the dirt around her filthy bare feet. Quiet sits between us for a moment before she speaks. "I can hardly wait to go home."

Home. She smells like she's been here for a while, so I figure she has been. "Where are you from?"

She eyeballs me for a second. "We don't really talk about things like that."

These people, I swear. "Things like what?"

"Where we come from." She looks at me hard and talks like I need to get the point.

I feel tired right away. *Buzz kill. Take a shower.* I could give a crap about what we do and do not talk about. "But you just said you can hardly wait to go home. I'm just wondering where that is, is all," I tell her back. The cup of tea warms my hands. This scene makes no sense.

"Oh, sorry, man," she laughs and backs off. "My bad. I was just talking about my tree."

Her tree?

"The one in the village. I've lived there for almost a year." A single dread falls forward over her shoulder, which she pulls back and ties around the rest of her rope-like hair. "I was just taking a break for a week and can't wait to get back. It's like home to me now."

This gets me. "You've lived in a redwood tree for a year?"

"We call her Indigo," she says. "Maybe you can visit if you decide to go to the tree sit."

My body loses its mad at this news. She's lived in it for a year. I've never thought of living in a tree. I just heart talk to them, share the same air somehow, but this girl knows redwoods in ways I have never even dreamed of. Now she's Tree Queen in my book.

I want to know if she talks to Indigo like I talk to Peter. And even though heights and getting arrested and aggressive loggers make going to the tree sit completely off-limits, I could visit if I want. I suddenly want to hold her hand and play with her hair. "Yeah, maybe," I lie. There's really no way because I'm leaving with the van the second it goes back to Portland. Still, sitting next to a real Tree Queen makes me giddy. "Do you talk to Indigo?" The words spill from mouth before I can pull them back in.

She smiles at me. "Why do you ask?"

"I'm just, you know, curious," I say quickly, before blowing and then sipping the spicy tea. Best to keep my mouth occupied before saying another word.

She looks a little on the spot and smiles. "Yeah. I do."

So much I want to know. "How does that work?" I can't help myself.

"Well," she says, "it's not exactly like we have a conversation. I just really feel her. I mean, she is alive, right?" Woodruff is not even being sassy, but says it like it is. She never wears her shoes when she's in the trees unless it's super bad weather, but even then she tries not to. Bare feet don't hurt the limbs and trunk as much as shoes can and it allows her to really feel the tree. She can feel if it's okay, if it's older or younger. Some trees seem really thirsty. Some welcome her. *Come hang*, they say. *I have lots of energy.* Others give off a strong *Don't be on me!* vibe, so she doesn't climb them. Some trees have branches or parts of the trunk that are dead, places too dangerous to climb, which she wouldn't really know unless she sensed it through her skin. "You can just feel it," she says. "Just like you can look at someone and know that they're sick or really healthy or kind." The longer she stays in a tree, the more she learns. "Do you talk to trees?" she asks. Of course she has to ask.

"No. No. I mean, no," I say because I don't know how to describe it. I don't even know what I'm talking to.

"Well, maybe you'll come meet Indigo," she says.

"Oh, I'm not staying long," I tell her. "I have to get back to Portland."

Woodruff glances at me sideways. "Suit yourself," she says before she picks up a nearby stick and inspects an insect crawling across the short length of it. "Look, I didn't mean to give you a hard time before." She points the stick toward the ground and the bug starts to work its way back to the damp earth. "But just so you know, we only talk about what people need to know here.

That's why we have forest names, to protect our identities. Our safety and the protection of these trees is at stake, and we don't share anything that could jeopardize that."

This makes perfect sense. "It's cool," I say and smile. She smiles back. Her smile is sunshine. I'm down with all this Need to Know. I've been the Queen of Need to Know since I left. I didn't mean to be Need to Know. I just had to be.

17

WOODRUFF AND JUSTIN HOP IN the van early in the morning to meet new kids who want to help at the sit. I figure I'll tag along, not really thinking, but just as we start to drive the alarm bells go off in my head. "Where are we going to meet these kids?" I ask, trying to sound cool.

"We're going to the co-op south of town," Woodruff yells back from the driver's seat.

South of town should be safe. It's far enough from Skatio, and I never go there. Neither does Liza because co-ops are for hippies. I tell myself this.

We pull into the long rectangular parking lot, and Daisy and Spore are sitting in the corner where no one is parked, on top of a big stuffed backpack with homemade patches sewn all over it. Daisy has fun choppy hair cut into a weird long Mohawk, and Spore has a crew cut. We all say hey to each other. They tell us they're travelers. I ask about Spore's name.

"He chose his name because he really is a fun-guy," Daisy says. She looks at the ground and snorts a laugh that says *I know that was dumb*, which saves her from being a complete dork. She has shiny brown eyes and a gigantic smile. Spore is either shy, tired of people asking about his name, or bored of her dumb joke, I don't know which. He pulls items from their pack one by one, trying to find something deep inside.

We all go into the co-op to get as much food and water as the crew can carry in their backpacks to the sit. They're going to run supplies tomorrow. Justin is stoned and I know this because he keeps walking up to the bulk food bins saying, "Oh my God! *This* would be *good*! Just look at how many things there are *in* there!" It's only trail mix with nuts and raisins, not even any chocolate chips. I tell him this. "You're the only sweet I need," he says, which I think is officially true after last night's cuddle fest.

Justin kisses the tip of my nose and runs his thumb along the NO MERCY cut that's still so sore my whole face hurts to move. His eyes track his thumb as it moves across my cheek, and his goofy grin, the one that always steals my heart, spreads across his face. Then he sees the food-sample table behind me where they're cooking mini sausages. "Whoa, look at *this!*" he says, grabs my hand, and pulls me over. We stand there, chowing down, just him Justin and me Mazzy being nowhere that matters except together.

The sausages are spicy and hot. Taking little bites helps to not hurt my cheek. We stand in the aisle near the meat counter, near the front of the store where posters are taped on the window—a fair, a 5k race, a fundraiser for some kid. A "Missing" poster. The overhead lights are very bright. I swallow. *Am I missing?* I want to see the poster. I don't want to see. *Am I on it?* My body is still, but now I don't move at all, not even to chew, suddenly worried that someone will notice me if I move. Ridiculous, really, as was the bright idea to go anywhere near town.

"I'm going to the car," I say with my mouth full, and I walk into some lady's cart with kids in it. Look down at the ground. "Sorry," I say, and I keep walking fast, not checking to see if Justin follows. *When is someone missing?* Out by the curb at the front of the van, heat comes off the grill of the car and smells like oil. I sit where no one can see me. Going with it all. What an idiot. I can't be missing yet.

Woodruff squeezes sideways between the van and the car

next to us. Four one-gallon jugs of water hang from her fingers, the kind the kid had at The What Not. They fall from her hands and clomp to the ground by her feet. "Freaking heavy!" She digs in her pocket for keys. "Ready for climb training?" she asks, and she loads the water into the side of the van.

"Yeah," I say, just to say something, and I jump in and sit with the plastic water jugs on the floor. Justin climbs onto the passenger seat and dives into the bag of trail mix. Spore and Daisy dump their stuff and squish in next to me. Woodruff stands outside the van, places one foot in the open door well, leans forward on her knee and explains how anyone who's climbing at the tree sit has to learn how to climb. The tree-sit vets are going to teach all the new kids how to do it. All I want is the van door closed.

Finally, we drive. Daisy talks non-stop, which is a relief because my brain is frozen stuck. *I can't be missing.* She goes on about how she became an anarchist because she had a broken heart because everywhere she looked and everything she heard she felt like people were never telling her the truth. Her talk starts to unstick my brain, and I follow every word away from that poster.

"That's the true definition of *anarchy*, you know. Instead of lies, I'm living by rules I think are true." She leans back against her backpack. "I'm making it up as I go." One hand lays on Spore's head in her lap, her fingers playing with the soft of his crew cut. She's the sweetest anarchist I have ever met, except that I don't think I've ever met one.

"I've never met an anarchist," I tell her. "Or none that I know of anyway."

"I'm your first anarchist?" She perks up at this news, her spine straight, her face brightened with a big smile.

"I think so," I say. Dressed-in-black, in-your-face freaks who draw weird symbols on their notebooks are what come to mind when I think of anarchists. She is nothing like that.

"That's rad," she says, her eyes scanning the outside world as it zooms by.

The farther we drive, the more I'm convinced that my face is not on some poster yet. I am definitely not missing.

We pull off in a teeny town where I've never been (population: fifty). Pepperwood? Peppergrove? Pepper-something. A handful of trashy homes line the road along with heavy-plastic-covered greenhouses, trailers with American flags, broken fences, rusted old trucks that look like they haven't been moved in a hundred years, one with no hood and a whole blackberry grove growing from the engine, old steel farming equipment, piles and piles of junk, Beware of Dog signs, and dirt roads that go off into places you can't see. We take one of those roads.

At the end of the winding driveway is a house that is as much falling down as it is still standing. We park and go around the side and through the wood gate that is held shut with an old bike tire that is slung over the posts. Woodruff is in charge and leads the way, and we all fall in line quietly because none of us really knows each other or what is going on.

The place is like some overgrown love fest that is either allowed to be overgrown with love or has just been forgotten about and every plant is trying to take over the world, left to be long and green and blowy. A little curvy path winds through it. The tops of fuzzy-headed grass come off easy in my fingers and the seeds blow away in the wind that is starting to turn wild. We all start to walk funny because the wind is so strong, each of us in our own little world. Daisy spreads her arms to each side like she's flying, and Spore moves his arms like he is doing the breast-stroke. If I yell, my words will blow back into my mouth. *I am not missing. I left.* Justin is quiet. His crash after flying, I guess.

There's a tent in one part of the big yard and a shack in another where it looks like people live. Woodruff tells us to wait while she goes to the tent and unzips the door, kneels down, and talks to somebody inside. We stand by a fire pit made from a rusted garbage can. Woodruff talks, looking kind of stressed, and glances back toward us. Nearby is a tree with one thick branch low to the ground that runs that way for a pretty long time before curving back toward the sky. It wants to be a bench, or have you lie on it like a cat on your belly and let your arms and legs hang off on either side. It wants you to *be* on it. *Be* with it. I'm sure of this. It's where I want to be, but Woodruff rezips the tent and walks right by us without saying anything. We follow her because no one knows what else to do. We walk past vegetable beds and a huge wood sign that is painted in big, dark blue letters: DON'T GROW OLD, GROW VEGETABLES. I love this place.

The climbing tree is a cedar with ropes wrapped around the trunk. Woodruff sorts the ropes, takes a big breath in, and says, "Okay," like *here we go again*, as if she's done this a hundred times before. Either that or whatever the person in the tent said really got under her skin. She demonstrates how to make knots, how to use a harness, and how to tie ropes from the harness to the bigger climbing rope that hangs from the tree. The bigger climbing rope is what you have to inchworm up. As she talks, we all sit in the strong California sun, which even in the fall gets to you straight through the chilly wind and makes you feel warm and dreamy, like living in honey. The more I sit, the more lazy-cat I get. I don't want to climb some tree. I just want to lie on the other one that's calling to me. *Jazzy. Jazzy. Jazzy.* This is when I know what my forest name will be.

Daisy is the first one up, and Woodruff helps her into the harness and then starts to connect various ropes.

"How do you get your forest names?" I ask because this part

isn't clear, but a nighttime naming ceremony with everyone sitting around a campfire definitely seems like it would be in the cards. A part of me secretly wonders what name I would be given.

"You just pick 'em and tell everyone," Woodruff says, like it's obvious, which bursts my bubble. She hangs her full weight on a hanging rope to test that it's secure.

The warmth of the sun mellows my body, legs stretched long, my fingers in the thick of the grass, my face toward the sky. A long-forgotten memory worms its way into my mind: I had my very own tree sit when I was about ten. I tell everyone the story.

My dad had plans to cut a tree in our yard. I didn't even really love the tree that much, too much leaky sap and ants. But there was no reason to cut it down, especially because he cut down so many other trees every day. So I sat in front of it and said I wouldn't move.

Dad yelled, "Birdie, get this kid away from the tree!" Mom tried to get me to move, but I wouldn't budge. An hour later Dad tried to talk me out of it, too. "Kiddo, this tree is just a pain. We got woods all around here!" I was committed, so they let me sit there all day. Even when it was time for dinner, I still wouldn't move. They ate without me and the sound of silverware on plates and talk escaped through the open windows. Dad told me no TV for the night, but no deal.

Mom finally called from the back door, "You win. Dad said he won't cut it down." She saved my dinner and told me to come in and heat my plate in the microwave. I was so happy that I went inside, psyched that the tree would stay. I sat down, and as soon as I took my first bite I heard the chainsaw.

"Oh my god, no way!" Daisy stops pulling on the ropes and hangs in the harness, her feet a few inches from the ground.

I ran outside crying, but Dad was already halfway through the trunk. I didn't talk to my folks for weeks.

Everyone at climb training is yelling, "No way!" Justin sits in the tall weedy grass next to me, puts his hand on my back, and rubs in circles. "Where's home, Maz?" he says, and he looks at me.

This question out of the blue. I am so on the spot that my face gets hot and red. "Need to know, my friend, need to know," I say, laughing, kind of making a joke, thinking I can't keep track. I'll tell him later.

"Oh," he says. "Need to know, huh?" His face gets weird and he looks away and laughs, too, but he doesn't think it's funny.

Woodruff tells me it's my turn. "Great!" I say, even though I'm sun lazy and have no plans of climbing at the tree sit. But I jump up anyway and shimmy into the harness.

18

AT DINNER I MANAGE TO GET my warm instant-pea-soup mush, plop down in the first camp chair, and heart say *Hi* to the giant trees. I won't move until I have to.

Climbing made me unbelievably sore because I have no stomach muscles and that and shoulders are what you need to get up that rope. We only had to climb about three feet today, and if I can't move now from three feet, I'd die on that rope for anything higher. They climb a hundred feet to live—ten stories high. There's no way. Plus the ropes and the harness hike your shirt when you climb. My belly and me are not into letting everybody see its flub, especially when it is all squished weird hanging in the harness. So not cool.

J-man was definitely bumming after climb training, but he wouldn't tell me what was making him quiet, even though I know. He ate his mush in two minutes flat and told everyone he was hitting the sack early. Such a fuzzy, cozy feeling came over me in front of the fire, and I could barely move, so I didn't go after him when he left. "Where are you going?" I called to his back, but he didn't answer.

Everyone sits around the fire pit, eating and talking, trying to decide what hippies are. No one agrees. Not one of these kids considers him or herself a hippie, but I would call at least half of them hippies. In our midst we have two traveling anarchists, Daisy and Spore, who is the gentlest anarchist I have ever met. He always has a spacey look on his face and takes a long minute to think before he says anything. And he sews! Woodruff is an activist and hates anyone thinking of her as a hippie because she "actually cares and does something," which I guess means that hippies don't. Justin is a weirdo, dorkbot, rant monster, love yummy, and is asleep. There's me—a not-missing, lying, lame wuss, who is friends with a tree and the daughter of a logger, which makes me what, exactly? And we have one cool-cat wanderer of the world. He's an old-timer tree sitter. Camp Grandpa, although he's not that old at all. He's a hippie for sure with a long ponytail and a beard and doesn't eat meat. Probably doesn't even own shoes. His woods name is Grey Goose, which comes from some song by a singer named Lead Belly about a goose that everyone keeps trying to kill, but the goose always gets away. Grey Goose sings and plays his banjo:

> *Last time I seen him (do do do),*
> *He was flying across the ocean (do do do),*
> *With a long string of goslings.*

The dense forest eats his banjo sounds while he plucks away and stares into the fire. We all sit snug and toasty and staring, too. I could get used to this, but I also can't wait to hightail it back to Portland. I am not ready to face anyone in Skatio. Not yet. Just one more day and I'll go back to my secret apprenticeship and my replant lovelies who need my love. I know I can't stay missing forever, so I'll figure things out from there.

Woodruff pipes up that it'll be time for shit duty when they get back to the tree village. Tree Queen Camp Mama, keeping everything running.

"Shit duty?" I ask.

"Yeah," she says. "We have to take the shit buckets and dump them." Blug. How do you poop in a tree anyway? Apparently I'm not the only one who wants to know. "That's the first question everyone asks when they want to know what a tree sit is like," Woodruff says.

And the answer is: shit bucket. Grey Goose explains that there's a shit bucket roped to the trunk and a branch on the tree. They climb down to it because it's roped in below where they sleep so they don't have to worry if they miss. They squat over it and "enjoy our animal pleasures" is what Grey Goose says, like he's talking about eating cake. So satisfied. When the buckets are full, they take them somewhere in the woods, dig super-deep holes, and dump them.

Lazy and achy in my camp chair, finally feeling good hanging with these kids, I tell them something I've never told anyone before. "I call pooping 'poovement,'" I say, kind of quiet, not believing that I've actually said it out loud. This gets everyone laughing. My stomach muscles and face hurt to laugh, but I can't help cracking up.

"Explain, my friend." Grey Goose puts another log on the fire. "What's your woods name anyway?" he asks.

"Just call me Jazzy," I say, and I say it like "Jaz-AAAAA."

"All right, Jaz-AAAAA," Daisy says. "What's 'poovement'?" This cracks me up even more because now other people are saying it.

Spore stares at the fire and says it, too, slowly. "Pooooovement."

My cheek is killing me.

When I was a kid I hated when adults said *bowel movement*, which seemed like something you should do with your shirt buttoned all the way to the top button. It didn't have the feel-good mooooove of a good poop. So I just combined *poop* and *movement*. *Poovement*. "The more ooooooo's the better," I explain.

"Now that's a word I can live with!" Grey Goose strums hard and fast on his banjo and improvises a bluesy poovement song:

One day I had a poovement, (bluesy strum)
Way up in a tree, (bluesy strum)
Cop told me, "Come right down."
I said, "Sir, can't you see?
I'm having a mighty fine poovement."

He sings it again, and everyone joins in this time.

After singing, talk keeps rolling—who's traveling where and when, who's allergic to what food, why coconut oil is good for you. I start the hippie talk again because I really want to know why everyone calls everyone else a hippie, but no one thinks they are a hippie.

Spore says that hippies are all Dead Heads.

Daisy says that hippies are people who just smoke a lot of pot and say, "Whoa, man," in a groovy way all the time. These hippies like to go to festivals and don't really do anything else.

Grey Goose says that there's no such thing as hippies anymore. They simply don't exist unless they are original hippies left from the sixties, still whacked on LSD. There are a few for-real hippies, but that's it.

Woodruff says that nobody wants to self-identify as a hippie. It's an apolitical term, and the whole identity is old.

I think what hippies are now are just other people that do things that annoy the crap out of you. Like when Daisy was hitchhiking and some mall chick with a blingy phone picked her up and called her friend and said, "I've got some dirty hippies in the car." If anyone is not a hippie it's Daisy the Anarchist, but since Daisy is not a mall chick, she's a dirty hippie to the real mall chick.

Dad and his buddies hate hippies. There are a few he's pegged around town that mostly he ignores, but they have a secret war going on. He and his buddies found a huge field of marijuana in the woods one day. They cut it all down, trying to be a pain to whatever hippies they thought were growing it. Whoever it was planted more somewhere else, and it turned into an ongoing joke. Loggers would find it, of course, because they know these woods better than anyone and can find anything here. They'd let the pot grow for a while and then out of the blue they'd go and cut it down again.

Anyone who tries to stop Dad from working is a "piece-of-crap hippie." All the "starry-eyed city kids who don't know a single thing about the woods and come here trying to tell us what's what." I didn't know what any of it meant. Dad was just a logger. That's what he did for work. But then there were these "pain-in-the-butt hippie kids" that were like cows that stand in the middle of the road when you're trying to drive and get somewhere—in the freaking way. Dad has had to travel hours for work when the land around town gets tangled in a lawsuit because of "these hippies." Or he won't have work for a while, which sucks for everyone if he can't work. His jaw muscles are always tensed, like he's chewing. He talks less and doesn't laugh when Mom says, "Well, now that you're around for a while you can help around the house." With stuff like me and Lily, the leaking roof, and getting the neighbor to fix the falling-down fence.

Work usually keeps him away from early in the morning. He comes home so tired he never has time for those things. He only wants to eat and drink with his buddies and watch some TV. Says he's earned the right. Everything else Mom has to deal with. He does take me fishing and camping when he isn't working, though. That's good. But when the "pansy tree-huggers" come to town, we don't even do that because he's too busy hanging at Gramps's place trying to figure how to get rid of them and save his job. They tell hippie jokes. "I wonder if we can light 'em on

113

fire with all that patchouli oil they wear." They laugh so hard, but they are so not joking.

How are all these smiling faces around the fire the people who make our lives suck so bad? Money so tight my folks fight all the time. Lily and me sneaking walks in the woods just to stay away from the house.

So many things are not adding up. All those hillsides where Dad told me they'd plant trees again when I'd ask why it was all gone. I believed him when he said that it's just the way things are, but I would look at the gray, sick color of the stumps and feel, *This is what sick looks like.* Thorny blackberry vines and poison oak the first thing to grow back. Plants that say, *Keep away! Don't come near me!* And trees everywhere, standing or cut, calling to me like ghosts. *Listen.*

It's just the way it is.

"I've heard it can get intense up there in the woods," I say, knowing what I'm talking about, wondering what these kids know.

"Yeah, it can," Grey Goose says. It gets quiet fast, just the crackle pop of the fire.

"You ever have to deal with a pissed-off logger?" I ask.

"Oh yeah. Yep. A few times," he says.

"What happened?" Daisy asks, and she lays down on a blanket looking at the tops of the trees that have been standing where they are for seven hundred, eight hundred, nine hundred years. Grey Goose tells his story.

He's at a tree sit somewhere, living a hundred feet high on a platform. They've been there for a while, mostly chilling in the trees. It was quiet and peaceful until one night, when all these loggers and forest-service guys they call "freddies" appear out of the blue. "You are on private land!" They yell into the trees using bullhorns. "You have ten minutes to come down, or you will be arrested!" Trucks on a nearby ridge blast lights into the woods.

Grey Goose yells down to them, "I'm sorry, but I can't do that. Not if these trees will get cut." People are running around on the ground that he can hear but can't see. There are kids in other trees. Kids hiding on the ground.

"One minute's gone," the freddies yell. "We're counting!"

His friends are yelling now too, "We love you! Hold strong!" to whoever is in the trees, their voices giving themselves away on the ground. Whatever happens, they yell so everyone can hear, praying someone has a camera or a voice recorder to record what is happening—"They're arresting me!" "owww!" "I'm not resisting, man!" "You don't have to stand on me!" "You just don't know when to quit, do you?"

Grey Goose doesn't know who's in the trees and who's on the ground. He hears movement in the branches, but he doesn't know who it is and he's not sure if he wants to know. It's darkest night. He takes a hammock that's stuffed in a bag on the platform and wraps himself in it. He connects the rope from his harness to a rope that's connected to another tree and lets himself fall from the platform and slides to in between. Kids are yelling down below, "Let me go!" He hangs in his harness and hooks the hammock so it's like a cocoon hanging down off the traverse line. He climbs in, shaking, and unties himself from the main rope, not even sure if any of the freddies see him, but kids on the ground know. They're yelling, "There are PEOPLE UP THERE! If you cut any line or any tree they will fall a hundred feet! Do you want them to die?"

They were in the way.

Then a chain saw drowns every sound. Grey Goose doesn't know where it is. He's hanging, crunched in a ball in the hammock cocoon. He doesn't know what's being cut. He's scared out of his mind. Is it the tree he'd been in? Is it the tree next to it that could fall into him? Is it branches below so kids can't climb down if they have no ropes, which gives them no choice but to be taken down by these guys? He has no idea but is sickened by the sound of cutting, his body shaking, getting ready to kiss four thousand tons of tree hello on his way down with it.

"I figure my life is a tiny thing compared to these trees that have lived for so much longer than any of us," he says, stroking his beard. "Those guys had no value for life of any kind, man."

It's just the way it is.

"What else will make it all stop?" Grey Goose says, simple and sure, and he pokes the fire. Eight hundred, nine hundred, a thousand years old is listening, too.

Spore finally breaks the silence. "That's intense."

Grey Goose stayed hanging in his cocoon and heard things falling around him. Branches, he figures. He waited for what felt like hours until kids getting arrested were taken away and most of the freddies and loggers were gone. It seemed quiet below, though he expected there were guys on the ground waiting for stragglers from the trees. Eventually he pulled himself through the dark across the rope and down another tree, and he ran away without being seen.

How did I really not know that there was another way?

116

19

J STARTS OFF THE DAY REALLY weird and doesn't even wake me. He's already sitting and eating when I go to breakfast. Grey Goose is all, "JAZ-AAAAA! Have you enjoyed your poovement today?" This is pretty funny, but J-man doesn't respond when I sit down next to him.

"So what's your name today?" he asks completely from left field. Weirdo.

"It's Jaz-aaaaa," I tell him, and I explain the silliness from last night.

He smiles. "Hmm," he says, and he takes a bite of oatmeal. I tell him I got his forest name. "Oh yeah?" He doesn't even seem interested.

"It's Jeremiad, dude! We decided for you." Grey Goose is the one who came up with it because he was listing his favorite words last night. *Jeremiad* is one. A *jeremiad* is a long rant about how messed-up the world can be. "Like Jeremy, only with an IAD on the end," is what Grey Goose had said. As soon as he said it I knew that was Justin's name, because that's what he does—goes off for hours about how the world should be instead of how it is.

"What do you think?" I ask him.

"What should I call *you* today?" he says like he didn't even hear me. "Is it Jazzy or Mazzy? Mazzy's cool. I like that. Or should it be something else?" He looks straight at me, which tweaks me because he's acting plain weird. But then he says, "Oh I'm just playing with you," and he smiles for real and takes a bite

117

of oat mush. That's when I start to feel like today is the day when it will all go down.

"Wanna go for a hike after breakfast?" he asks.

Yes. Yes I do.

We start on a hike after washing dishes. I'm debating whether I'll bring him to Jedediah. Jade/Jazzy/Justin/Jeremiad/Jedediah. All these *J*s. Not long into our green walk Justin starts doing his jeremiad thing about how these are the only old trees left and how there's only 3 percent of what used to be here. Giant redwoods live like little separate islands all over the coast, and there's no more vast areas of redwood forest. How these money-hungry logging companies still don't have enough yet, and how there are twenty things he'd rather be doing than taking them on. But no. "There's no choice anymore. There's NO CHOICE!" he shouts to the treetops.

I've never really seen him so amped up, and I'm wondering what the hell is going on. Since when was he taking anything on, first of all? He said we'd just camp. And second of all, it's only morning. Chill.

He's going off. "Will they ever stop? No. It's not enough for them to cut every single thing around them because clear-cutting's cheaper and easier. 'Let's just cut all the giants down at once,'" he mimics what he thinks they sound like. "Freaking loggers." Justin walks fast now, practically yelling. "Don't they think for themselves? Don't they ever stop to think for just one second that the herbicide they use to kill the weeds on a clear-cut is just too much?"

There's something else in his going on, and I can't figure what it is. So loud. Too many words. Maybe he's listening to too much talk at camp. Whatever it is, his freak-out gets under my skin because this is not about talking to each other. It's about something else that I don't know yet. And sure, what he's saying is right, but it's getting to me because Mr. "We're Going North" doesn't have a clue that my dad is one of those loggers he's going on about. If there's anyone who thinks for himself, it's my dad. It's not like he has no brain, like he just takes orders.

"He's a single jack faller, you loser," is what I want to say. "Gramps called them the orneriest bastards in the forest, you know! You don't even know what one is!" A logger going into the woods on his own to cut down a tree all by himself because he can't stand working for the man, how serious hard and killer dangerous it is, making his own rules and still making a living. More than Justin can say for himself. "How long have you been going to college now? Five years or something? Have you ever had a job?" I want to ask him. "Oh, and this has nothing to do with anything, I know, but how many music festivals have you been to recently? With what *friends*? How many *friends* do you have, anyway?" I'm having this conversation all by myself, and Justin's having his conversation all by himself. Nine-hundred-year-old trees listening to all of it.

I'm looking right back at them. *What?*

Justin's going on, "How do loggers have the balls to take these trees down with the one thing they cannot protect themselves from? Fire? Floods? Bugs? Earthquakes? No problem. They've figured out how to survive all that forever. Chainsaws? Redwoods can't do a thing about those. It's like shooting someone in the back. I mean, look at those Doug firs!" he says, and he points at some trees.

"Those are redwoods," I say, thinking, *You are so dumb.*

"I know redwoods," he says. "I'm talking about those." He points again.

"Those are noble firs," I tell him. Duh.

"Noble, huh?" This stops him because he clearly doesn't know his Doug fir from his noble fir.

"Look at the needles!" I walk over and point to how nobles have needles that are stiff and silver green. Douggies have needles that are softer and darker. That's how you know.

"Is that so?" he asks.

"I could tell you, like, seven hundred things about trees," I say, which is almost true.

"And how do you know this stuff?"

"I just like evergreens," I tell him, which is true enough for now, because if he keeps his freak going, today is not the day we're going to talk. Plus we haven't found a place to sit yet.

"Evergreens," he yells, and he runs ahead of me. "Evergreens, we love you!" He runs with his arms out like he's giving everything a giant hug. Cute jerk. Moody freak. I want to walk away right then. His yell in these woods is way too loud. He *is* that city kid who doesn't have a clue. He runs ahead, and I see Jedediah off to the right. Jeremiad. Jedediah.

"Hey," I say, and I turn down that path. "Come see this tree." I'm not sure it's such a good idea, and then I know it's not a good idea when he runs right past me.

"That one, Maz?" he yells, and he runs right into the thousand-year-old middle of Jedediah, like he doesn't even have to ask.

Now it's me who's yelling. "What are you doing?" Justin running right into Jedediah like he's some bouncy house. "You can't just do that!" He's already inside, climbing and then standing on where the elephant-wide trees are all joined together, looking down at me.

"Do what?" he says like it's not obvious.

"These trees are not a jungle gym, you idiot!" My cracked cheek is sore from stretching.

"Whoa," he says, and he squats down. "What is your problem?"

"My problem is that you run around and yell and say *anything you feel like*. You don't even know what you're talking about. Do you hear yourself? Do you think any of these trees rant?" I don't care if I make no sense. "Trees do not rant. Look at these trees! Don't just run into them. LISTEN TO THEM!"

Justin is all daddy longlegs, squatting on the coming-together parts of the tree. "All right, freak," he says. "That's more than you've talked to me in two whole days." He jumps down and walks over to right in front of me. We stare at each other. "You want me to listen?" he says. "Okay. I'll listen. And when we're done listening to the trees, you're going tell me what's going on."

It's time. I know, but instead I say, "We're just friends, right? So I don't really know how much there is to talk about." Really what I want is to be tangled in his twiggy elbow arms. He half turns his curly, brown-gold head and looks at me for a long minute from the corner of his eyes, and I don't look away. He smiles a little. I try not to, but I laugh. I'm mad. "You're a jerk," I tell him.

"You're a freak," he says, and he grabs my hand and I let him. We sit on a bench by the trail to listen, but today of all days the tourists decide that it's time for a hike. It must be the weekend. They've been walking by us, but I didn't really notice. Sitting, I see them all.

There's a huge tree as long as about five or six eighteen-wheeler trucks lying on the ground nearby, maybe fifteen hundred years old. It fell down forever ago. Knotted roots like tangled veins form one giant root ball that stretches twenty-feet high with the tree on its side. People walk by, and even though there is a sign that says, DO NOT WALK ON THE TREE, at least four different groups climb the giant trunk. Japanese tourists take pictures. Some kid yells to his dad walking on the dinosaur, "We could carve our names into it!" A smart girl walks from the top of the tree all the way down to the roots and says,

"Am I walking back in time?" She's trying to tell her father what walking back in time would look like, but he is already far ahead of her. She yells after him, "Would you wait? You're always in such a hurry!"

Justin can't help himself and whispers really loud. "Grey Goose told me yesterday that redwood roots only go down in the ground about ten feet, maybe twenty." I nod my head I know. "They stay standing because they hold on to other tree roots." I nod my head I know again. "Doesn't that blow your mind? They all look like they're standing on their own, but they're all massively connected right under our feet!" I look at him and put my finger to my lips. He doesn't know how to listen.

A family walks by holding video cameras and wearing weird clothes—girls and women in long dresses with aprons and little hanky hats and men with weird beards. One snorts and then spits. "This is like Jurassic Park!" he says.

Justin whispers again. "You know what else Grey Goose told me?" He can't shut his trap. "The Japanese have this word, *shinrin yoku* or something. You know what it means?" I shake my head. "Dude, it means 'forest bath.' Like the whole forest cleans your soul or something. Isn't that rad?" This makes perfect sense to me, sitting there trying to soak in it. But then the guy with the weird beard says, "This tree is worth a million bucks every hundred feet!" He ruins it. He starts doing the math in his head as he walks. "This tree is worth at least three or four million bucks!"

This is not the kind of listening I'm talking about. Finally, everyone shuts up, and we sit for a while.

"So, Jazzy," Justin says when Jurassic family is gone.

"Just call me Mazzy," I say because somehow today hearing *Jazzy* out loud in front of this tree sounds wrong. I'm so *not* Jazzy, and it knows it.

"You know what?" He turns to me, and his eyes are serious.

"You tell me I don't listen, but you know what? You never really say anything."

Out loud, I'm thinking. *I do to you, Peter.* And in my notebook, but not out loud. Not that much. This is true.

I want his eyes to be home again. I want them to invite me in, and so I start to tell him some things I haven't told him. Details. Things he wants to know. That I freaked on the first day because I used to live really close to here, two towns away in Skatio, and I had no plans, thank you very much, of being back here this soon. My head couldn't make sense of it at first. I told him how I left here and how I wasn't ready to see anyone. Not yet. How I didn't leave my folks a note. How maybe they're looking for me. Liza too. I don't know. How I have a little sister, Lily, who must be so, so sad. How much I miss her. And that my dad is a logger and cut half the hillsides down around here. How this, more than anything, broke my heart and made me not be able to stay because he said it would all grow back, but it didn't. Not in the same way. How I didn't know what to do, so I left. About how I am so wrong for leaving because leaving isn't doing anything to change things, but I didn't know there was anything to do. I didn't know that then. I just couldn't stand listening to any more lies.

So much more wants to be said, sitting in the silence of the woods, Justin's soft, green eyes on me, listening. For everything I tell him, there is so much I don't—Peter, NO MERCY, that day at The What Not. What I don't dare say sits in my heart like rocks across a river, things I could step on to get to the other side, if I would only say them aloud. But I don't.

"Anyway," I say instead, "my real name is Jade. Mazzy is my hiding name. I didn't want anyone knowing where I was until I figured out what I was doing."

"Jade, huh?" Justin looks at me for a while, like he's trying to decide what to say. "I don't know," he finally says, "I think I like that name best of all." He wraps a long arm around me. My head finds its favorite place on his chest bones, some of my secrets no longer only in me, but now living between his heart, the trees, and me. We sit that way for while until he breaks the silence. "Jade, I think we're more than just friends. Don't you?"

I've said enough for now. I'll save more for later. And I am so ready to be welcomed in his eyes again. "Mm-hmmm," I say. "Yes, I do."

We walk kissy, wandering, and slow back to camp, where we're smiley and mushy. Justin will help with the supply run tomorrow and visit the tree village for the day. I'll stay and help at camp. We get to go back to Portland when he comes back down tomorrow night. And then all we are is together.

20

ON THE 101 I THUMB FOR a RidE, shaking mad. Mad in my bones, moving my body, walking me north. I'm practically running I'm walking so fast. The rhythm of my feet walking. Justin sucks. He freaking knows everything.

Sitting in my sleeping bag, going through things in the tent this morning, this paper falls from my notebook when I empty my backpack:

I NEED TO KNOW

Justin's all sleepy-face mush in his pillow. "What's this?" I ask, thinking it's some cute note.

He opens his eyes, and his face freezes. "I didn't know what was going on with you. You were acting so weird." He's talking nervous. "I was going to tell you. I just didn't know how."

"Tell me what?" I ask, not getting it at all.

"I read it, Maz. I read it." He can barely speak. The tent is tiny. My head pushes against the slant of the roof. "The other night when you were hanging at the campfire, I wasn't in here sleeping," he says, but he doesn't say another word. He looks like he's going to cry.

My ratty spiral notebook is in my hand. I'm getting it now. He's telling me this. I have to get out. What does he know? Everything. I'm grabbing things, maybe they're mine, maybe not. I shove them in my bag. That's why he was so freaky. He knows everything. He kneels, his head pushes against the top of the tent too, and he tries to block my way. "You gave me all that 'need to know' BS!" he says like it's all my fault.

An unreal mad erupts from way down deep in my gut. "Who said I want you to know anything?" I yell and haul off and shove him hard right in his boney chest, like a punch. He falls back. My hands shake trying to get the damn zipper up. I get it half-way, and it jams. I grab each side and try to tear it open, but it stays jammed. Throw my backpack to the ground and shove my way out, worried that my hair will get caught in the zipper. I crawl through the opening and walk and run and walk and run. Who cares what happens.

It's foggy and chilly and early, and there are not many cars on the road. Search my memory for what I wrote, but what's happened and where I've been is a blur. A green pickup truck slows down ahead of me. It could be my neighbor, or my dad in a borrowed truck for all I know. I'm so screw-it that I open the door and step from one world right into another one. Just like that. The truck-cab smell is so familiar—weird mix of chainsaw oil, gas, and wood sap.

The soft of my hood is good to hide inside because it drapes over my face, which I keep turned toward the door. Sneak a quick look at the driver, but can't see much. Don't look twice. Cough while I talk and tell him to drop me off on the 101 on the other side of the bridge leaving town. The landscape passes quickly as we pick up speed. All I want is to settle into silence with Peter. *Here I come.* The walls of my world all falling away. My finger on my hand, resting on my leg, tapping my knee. What did I write about that day at The What Not?

There is so much farmland here. Lots of pastures running down off hills that are all patchy like a quilt; some squares are cut and brown and others are fuzzy with green grow-back. Then I see what I cannot believe. The Skatio Lumber Company sign is gone. That sign was like God looking down on everyone. The mill runs right through the center of Skatio, and you could see the sign from the highway—way longer than a football field, with huge blocky letters reminding everyone who's in charge.

I have to know. "Why'd they take the sign down?" I ask, and suddenly I remember this guy is Ed. Just my luck. Gramps's buddy who always talks about the old days, whenever they were. He never pays much attention to me, and I pray with everything I have that he doesn't notice me now. He doesn't seem to, or if he does he's not letting on. If he did recognize me he'd have said something by now, and the whole town would know in two minutes flat. His guts fills the space between him and the steering wheel.

"Well. The sign's down because the town is for sale now," he says, and then he goes off. Yep. A hundred years of company-town life thrown away for some kind of sale because some corporation in Texas doesn't know a crawdad from a redwood. Bought the town with junk bonds, not even real money, clear-cut the hills, and still had no money. Didn't take care of anyone that was working for them. Not like it used to be when it was family-owned, which it was for like eighty years. There was respect. Respect for the land. Never logged more than they could replant. Respect for the people who worked there. Texas bigwigs don't know a thing about how much to take. They just take it all until there's nothing left and somehow don't know how to even balance their books. But none of it matters now. Barely any land left to log, crack-head environmentalists getting legal about anything that's left and him out of a job, which he was planning on quitting anyway. What with the price of timber in the toilet and the corporate way that just made no sense. Cutting more trees with smaller teams, which was more dangerous and near impossible. The days of a man alone with a tree long gone. The art of it. Knowing how to make it fall in exactly the right spot you want it to. A whole way of life just gone.

I know this speech by heart because it's the one Dad was always making to Mom about why he would never in a million years go work for SLC. It's why he never wanted to live in Skatio, but next door in Rodell, because Dad just couldn't take the whole company-town thing. But Mom never got it. She was raised there and couldn't understand who wouldn't want everything taken care of by people you've known your whole life. "But that's just it," he'd say to her. "You don't know the people who are running that place anymore. They're not from here, and what do they know or care about you?" He didn't trust them as far as he could throw 'em, is what he said. "I don't know, Birdie, but it's gonna fall one day. I'm telling you. This full-of-beans company and this town, it's gonna fall."

How much does a town cost, anyway? Who buys it?

Ed going on, and, even though the huge sign is down, everything else looks the same. The giganto piles of cut and bark-stripped logs at the mill. I want to go over and push them. Watch them roll down from the rolly piles, like I could free them or something, only it's too late because they already lost their roots. Stacks of wood. Two-by-fours weathered black like they haven't moved in years. They used to look so fresh-cut, but these haven't moved. The giant mill that is big and butter yellow sitting right on the river. The little grid of company houses all looking the same. Fifty? One hundred of them? Tiny town. All those little houses with their little front porches. The mill choking smoke into the air.

A logging truck passes us. Dead logs chained together. Bark ripped where the chains are holding them down. Spray-painted numbers on the end: 32-A. 33-B.

Ed so does not know who I am. I'm just some kid on the road

he's giving a ride to who's stuck in his truck and has to listen. Some no one with nowhere to go. "I wonder if it's gonna end up like Falk?" I say. Funky little mill ghost town left in the hills from a hundred years ago. I make myself sound stuffy like I have cold, just in case. Ed's not even listening because he's still going on about how he doesn't understand his buddy who lost his hand and won't even use his disability. That'd make sense maybe if it was years ago, but he won't make a claim against these thieves all because he feels he should have known better. Like it was his fault losing his hand. Too proud. But Ed keeps telling him, "Take these bastards for everything they got because they're taking everything from you!" But no, his buddy goes and rigs his own fake hand because he's a technical kind of guy and can do that stuff, and he goes right on working. "You mind if I make a quick stop?" he says like its part of his story.

"Sure," I say because Justin's ruined everything and mad is all that's in me now. Mad calling the shots. But then Ed cuts across the highway quick to make it in time for the exit I thought we would pass. It looks like I am going to town. He pulls off right, goes around the off-ramp loop, and then we're heading on the road west toward my house. If he keeps going straight, it will not be good. I change my mind. "Where are you going?" I ask. I'll tell him to drop me off right here. Any closer and I risk running into Liza.

"I'm just feeling thirsty," he says. "I'm going to get me a lemonade. You want one?" He slows down to make a left. He's not heading west, but driving straight down Main Street in Skatio. Lemonade. I can't get dropped off here, right in the middle of everything.

"I'm cool," I say, and I slump down and pull my hood tighter around my face. The truck will be a good place to wait. The town is up for sale. The What Not must be jammed with loggers trying to figure out what comes next. Ed turns into the BiMart parking lot, and no matter where he parks, I could find my way into that store with my eyes closed. I've been into it a million times. He parks his truck in the back corner of the lot.

"You coming in?" he asks.

Look out my window. "Nope," I say. The lawn guy is cutting the grass at the old hotel. "I'll wait."

"Suit yourself," he says, and he gets out and slams the door. The truck starts cooling off, the engine makes clicking sounds, settling down. There is no one in the parking lot that I can see who can see me. Ed walks to the market, the sliding door opens, and BiMart swallows him whole. The sealed-off quiet in the truck.

How much of everything does Justin know? Nelson and Gramps drinking beers on the porch. Johnny Cash shot the guy in Reno. The sound of the chainsaw. How I didn't do one single thing to stop them. Or save that kid.

A burgundy minivan parks one row away and fives spaces down. A mom gets out, yanks her child from the back car seat, stands her up on the pavement, takes her by the hand, and drags her inside.

Sitting in this truck, just waiting to be seen. I'd have to tell them everything I saw. Did I write it all down? Ed's taking way too long.

I can't wait anymore.

The truck door needs a shove to open. I slide from my seat, and walk across the parking lot to Main Street. The road's not that long. It's just a day. If anybody stops me, I'll say I've been camping, or visiting friends in Portland for a while. That's all. I'm not missing. There's an old steam locomotive stuck in the lawn in front of the old hotel. What's going to happen to the old hotel now? A car rounds the bend just ahead and drives right toward me, slowly, like the driver's looking for the right address, or scanning the area for something. It's just a day. *The Skatio Sentinel* newspaper box sits in the grass next to the sidewalk. I open the metal door, and it creaks. Inside the box is a stack of newspapers. I grab one, which gives me something to do. The car passes. I let go of the door, and it slams shut. Drop my backpack to the ground, shove the paper in, sling it back over my shoulder, sink my fists into my sweatshirt pockets, and walk. It's just a day. Justin got me into all of this. I walk until I see the overpass, walk under it, to the other side, to where the highway meets the woods. Cars zip by. It's not far to the trees. Not far until I'm gone.

21

I FOLLOW THE EEL FOR ALMOST an hour. Away from town, away from cars, away from people. My body craving the cool quiet of my Family Circle. *Almost there!* I walk, not seeing anything, until floppy fish catch my attention. It's baby-making time for salmon. Crazy how they do this every year, swim all the way home from wherever they've been in the ocean. They come back, lay eggs, and then die. What's that about? I sit on the riverside rocks and watch as they fight their way upstream only to get thrown back down in a current and then wiggle their bodies back up again. So much work. What can they possibly think they're doing? Don't they know they're going to die?

I wouldn't do it. I'd wave to all the other dumb fish swimming upstream and say, "See ya, suckers!" and let the river take me right back to the ocean. I'd float, flip upside down, look at the sky and the treetops. Salmon only ever see the ground.

Not many at all this year. One wiggles itself out of the river and up a dry creek bed. Isn't that just it? *No more water that way, dumb-o!* The fish flops itself in that direction anyway, because its got to do what its got to do. Doesn't even know it's headed for dry land.

Watching it struggle its way to its own death is more than I can take. The river rocks are unsteady beneath my feet as I make my way over to pick it up. No sooner is stink fish in my hands then I realize that this is even dumber—now I have blood on my hands. There are bears in these woods, and they smell everything. That would be cute. Me alone with Peter, bloody, sitting there for a bear to come snack on me. All for some half-dead fish.

The salmon is big, close to two feet, with skin coming off from hitting against too many jagged rocks, rubbing off on my clothes now, and me. The fish fights, thrashing like one giant muscle trying to get out of my arms, like I'm getting in its way. *I'm trying to help you!* I carry it over the slippery stones to where the icy Eel flows. Salmon swim from three thousand miles away in the ocean and might not ever make it home. That would *suck*. The fish flings itself from my grip and back into the river, and the flow pulls it right back downstream, before it starts jumping upriver again.

"You're going the wrong way!" I yell, splashing water on my arms, trying to wash it all off me.

Every bend of the old logging road Dad and I used to use is so familiar—where mushrooms grow in the fall, where wild purple iris grow in the spring, where elk hang super early in the morning. I run along the trail, happiness practically bursting from my chest at the chance to be alone with these woods. Not with hippies. Not with Justin. Not with trouble.

The path is etched in my head: turn right as soon as I reach the top, where an old clear-cut has filled in, pretending to be a real forest; then turn left and follow that trail a bit before turning left again at the ridge; walk just a little farther until the Circle of Giants.

I finally get to be with you, Peter!

Running uphill in the foggy fall morning, things start to look different. Before I even make it to the top of the ridge twisted stumps and pointy, wooden spikes mar the ground where trunks were torn away. *Am I at the right ridge?* Rewalk the road in my head—mushroom hillside, iris spot, elk morning hang. Turn.

I'm at the right spot.

Giant trees still stand on the ridge and I try to run through what looks like dried, gray driftwood. Peter must be at the top, where it's still lush and old and quiet. *Tell me they only took the skinny trees!* I got my areas mixed up. That's all. Clumpy earth is turned up in spots, and drops way down in others, and makes the ground uneven. Weird, scrubby plants and thorns scratch at my shins. Logs and broken branches, shards of tree longer than me, poke as I try to get by. I can't move fast enough, up and over, through the mess, past the one tree standing in the middle of nothing stumps. I'm all heartbeat and no breath. I must not be remembering right.

At the top of the clear-cut, big trees look out over what's left. I run into what still stands and ferns hit me like a wave, like seaweed, the ground spongy beneath my feet. A few massive trees stand together farther down the ridge and I wade toward them, green up to my armpits, the sweet-smelling damp and wild forest in tact like it's always been. Cool, clean air opens the inside of my nose and the all-around ocean-forest is a hush, except for the sound of water dripping on leaves. The closer I get, the more I'm sure. Sucking in air, my heart pounds against my ribs. Those trees are not my Family Circle. I turn around and look back over hard, crusty dirt and so many stumps, all in a perfect square patch.

My chest feels hollow, my head dizzy. I don't know where to put myself. A giant stump is the only flat place to sit and I clomp through the cloying ferns, making my way toward it, scanning the dry, torn-up nothing-left for any sign of Peter, but nothing is familiar. No Family Circles to see what grows together, what trees go together. My backpack drops with a dull thud to the ground and I sink down to the stump that holds all of me, curled in a ball, cheek against rough cut, looking sideways at the world.

Small gasps break up my breathing, as if I've been punched in the gut. There's nowhere to look that doesn't have this view.

Twenty minutes pass, maybe more. I can't move. I try. Maybe an hour. Two? I tell myself to move, but I don't. I tell myself to get up. I don't.

Birds dart around and make a racket, upset about something. A giant, dark bird cuts across the clear-cut and heads right for the one tree left, where it lands with a screech. A red-tailed hawk, perched on a branch, taking it all in.

The damn bird just looks at me. "WHAT ARE YOU STARING AT?" I push myself up to sitting and yell, but its not even words that leave my body now, but big, ugly, mean sounds that come from way down deep in my gut. Every wrong decision I've made. How much is lost. How there's nowhere to hide. I push it out like it's something that can leave my body, until the sound is thin, mixed with breath and then nothing. The hawk doesn't even look away. The trees keep their silence. The sky grows dark and I lay back down on the stump. The van is heading home. I have to get back.

Dad and I sat somewhere on this ridge once, not far from this spot, back when he told me everything he knows about the woods. He explained how when a tree falls, it doesn't die. Not really. It turns into a nurse log, home for all kinds of critters and plants living off it, new trees sprouting from the roots of what fell. And before it goes, the tree sends all of what makes it alive, all of what it uses to save itself from bugs and sickness during its life, down into its skinny roots and gives it to the trees around it. Like a message. It gives what's left of its life to the world that keeps on living, and the other roots take this up. All this giving to each other underground. Dad would talk about it like it was the most magical thing in the world. His dark eyes bright like he was telling me a fairy tale. "The life just jumps, kiddo, from one tree right to the next," he said. "Life in the woods keeps going on and on. It never stops."

I slide the lump of me off the edge of the humongous stump and kick away sticks and chunks of wood until there is a clear, round patch of dirt. Down on my knees, I dig. The topsoil is hard and dry, but it's not far until the cool and moist underneath. I make my hands into a scoop and pull dirt to one side to start a pile. My hands are small and don't hold much. I keep digging. I don't feel whatever it is that jumps around down there, from tree to tree. The pile of dirt gets bigger even though most of it tumbles down the side, back into the hole, mixed with twigs. Night coming makes everything almost the same color dark.

My tin should be somewhere around here, deep in the ground, with all those letters. I wrote so many. I wouldn't even know where to look.

When the hole is deep enough, I pull the spiral notebook from my backpack and open it to the back flap, where the secret compartment is. It's hard to get my hand in because of how tight it's taped. I did that on purpose. The cardboard scrapes my knuckles as I feel around the different papers for the one with the corner torn off the top of the page, the one I started to write to Peter or Lily or my parents about why I left. I was going to send it. I haven't finished it yet. The letter slides out easily. I lay it at the bottom of the hole, and push all of the dirt back in on top of it. I don't want to carry it around anymore.

22

MY FEET ARE MY EYES now, feeling my way in the dark. Can't see much except the wide, rocky clearing of the road, tall forest on either side, a slice of moon. One foot in front of the other. I tell myself what I know. *Air that I breathe. Roots beneath my feet hold it all together. Home to so many things.* Big, weird piles block my way. I can't walk a straight line for the piles that look like wood stacks for a bonfire.

Did I really believe they wouldn't take you, too?

A weird sound comes from the woods. I freeze. It's quiet for a minute or two, and I'm about to walk when it comes again. "Hoot! Hoot!" It's a wannabe *hoot* from some person. Have I been hearing it for a while now? Walking on what's probably private land, it could be freddies. I could get arrested. I should hide, but I've been on this land my whole life and didn't worry about it then. Sad fills the inside walls of my chest. Do I really have to hide?

"Hoot! Hoot!" comes again. Freddies don't hoot. The sound of running feet, crunching leaves and sticks. I turn to face whatever's coming for me. A dark body jumps from the woods onto the road.

"Jazzy, man. What are you doing here?" Grey Goose whispers loud. "You gotta get off the ground." I try to tell him that I'm just trying to get back to camp, but he pulls me into the woods, walking fast through skinny little trees.

"I just went to meet a friend," I say. Our whispers and

stepping sounds are so loud in the night. "I'm from here. I can walk around if I want, can't I?"

"No, you can't, man. It's been crawling with freddies today."

"What are they gonna say?" This sounds way feistier than I mean it to. I'm only asking a question. "I'll just tell them I went to meet a friend in the woods, but I didn't see him. That's the truth."

Grey Goose turns back to me. "Yeah. You're friends with us, and if you're caught, that means we're busted, too. Come on," he grabs my hand and pulls me. "This isn't some booty-call visit for some of us, Jazzy."

"Booty call?" I stop in my tracks. "Is that what you think I'm doing out here?" I am not quiet about this. He doesn't say anything but keeps tromping forward. "I know these woods better than any of you!" is all I can think to say. "And I am not Jazzy!"

"Shhhh!" he says. He turns around, comes back, grabs my hand again, and starts moving fast. I don't want to get anybody busted, so I move fast, too, keeping pace, stepping in his footsteps. I may know these woods better than him, but not that well in the dark. "Jazzy or Mazzy or whatever the hell your name is, we've just got to get off the ground."

I try and tell him that I'm going to call myself Jade now, make him understand this is no booty call, but I don't bother. He's not listening. It's dark, and I want to get back to the van. I fall quiet into walking, talking to myself, naming the only things I actually know. *Redwood trees don't have sap.* Things my dad told me. *One-tenth of 1 percent of all the seeds that fall actually grow into trees. The rest are eaten, pooped out, drowned, or blown away.*

"Where you been, anyway?" he whispers back over his shoulder.

"I told you, I'm from around here." I'm done with secrets and stupid forest games. "I went to see a tree I love," I say. The fact of no Peter slaps me in the face. "You know what?" I say because Grey Goose will actually get it. "They cut it down." Saying it out loud doesn't make it real.

He stops and turns around, and I walk right into him. "They cut it?" he says. I step back and look into his shaggy face and nod my head. "Dude. I am so sorry." He gives me a big hug. I let him hold me. His smell is sweat and spicy. "I am so sorry," he says again. "Come on. We'll feed you." He moves fast again in the back woods, and I'm tripping over branches. We walk quietly for a while until he says, "Okay. Here we are."

It's not camp. It's I don't know where. A long rope hangs down from some huge tree, and he tugs on it and yells, "Woodruff! Jazzy's here! I'm taking her over to Everlast!"

She calls back, "I'll meet you over there!"

I am not climbing, and I tell him this. "And I am not Jazzy." I tell him again.

He gets serious. "You have no choice, man. It's dark and it's not safe. You shouldn't even have been walking around." He's acting like this is it. "Come on." He moves fast and looks around like he's worried. "All they need is to find you down here, and you could get us all nailed." There's another super-wide tree with a rope hanging down. "They were all around here today. They wouldn't talk to us, but they were definitely checking things out." Nelson. "We'll find someone to take you back down on Saturday, but not tonight. They could still be working tonight." He hands me a harness.

Oh my good god. Saturday is two days away.

Grey Goose reminds me about everything. The chest knot. The foot knot. The stirrup. What not to do. I can't remember anything. I put on the harness. He attaches my ropes. He puts his headlamp on me so I can see. He's going to climb a few trees

139

away and keep an eye on me. Woodruff will be at the top. I wonder where Justin is. Grey Goose hangs on the rope to test that it's connected right. "These ropes can hold, like, three elephants," he says. This is meant to make me feel better. Three elephants. "You'll be fine just as long as you're off the ground. You'll make it," he says, and then he yells, "She's coming up!"

I lean back in my harness, and the rope has so much stretch that I sink almost down to the ground. It's going to be a long night. I stand in the stirrup, slide my chest knot as high as I can on the rope, lean back in my harness, and slide my foot knot up and then grab the rope, step into the stirrup again, and hoist my whole body, just like he said. Three elephants. I do it again. Chest rope. Harness. Foot knot. Stirrup. Haul my whole body. Do it again. And again. I try not to swing too much. I do. I try not to crash into the tree. I do. All the way up.

I do this forever and then look down. I'm only about ten feet off the ground. Ninety more to go. I am going to cry. I haven't even reached the first branch yet. All I can barely see is giant wide trunk and the bottom of Grey Goose, who is already halfway up his tree. *Stupid Grey Goose, you jerk!* I want to yell. I'm going to tell him that I'm hiking back down and won't get nabbed by any freddies. I know the back places, where to go. But, the fact is, I'm really not that sure. I want to do it anyway, but there's no way. It's the rest of these kids and these trees. It isn't just me.

I keep climbing. I hate it. I have to make it to the top. There's no choice. I hate it. Anger at every single thing floods my body— fear of being on the rope, who's below that wants to yank me down, life in the tree village and whether I can hack it. The only reason I'd do any of it is gone.

This time the fact of no Peter takes over and I'm suddenly all tears. I sit back in the harness, hold on, and cry. Stuck on a rope. My dorky headlamp lights all these places that nobody ever sees—the branches, needles, and leaves of trees twenty or thirty feet high.

"How you doing down there?" Woodruff whispers.

"I don't know," I yell back and use my shoulder to wipe the snot from my face.

"Shhhhh!" Someone shushes me.

"You gonna make it?" Woodruff whispers again.

"I don't know," I whisper yell, too. Damn the jerk who shushed me.

"You will," she whispers. "Take your time. You'll make it."

I don't know.

The burn of blisters start to raise on my fingers and I'm only about a third of the way up this rope that three elephants can hang from without breaking it. Silence surrounds us. *This is stupid. A rope is just a rope. Three elephants are three elephants and I'm just hanging here.* The super-wide trunk that grows toward the sky like it always has is so solid. I get a hit of how old. Six hundred years? I am no elephant. I'm more like a spider, an elephant spider. This tree they call Everlast is holding me, and then I get it: *this tree is not going to let me down.*

It's a crazy feeling hanging from a thread, hanging from a tree. I'm so screw-it that I let go and fall back and hang from the harness at my hips. My legs, my arms, and my head all hang upside down in a frown. This is what the world looks like upside down—you can talk yourself into trusting the one thing that's holding you up.

Tears fall from my face to down past where the light from my headlamp ends. There are at least sixty more feet to climb, maybe more. Who knows what time it is. Nine o'clock maybe. This gets me going. So much climbing juice in my blood by now. My deal with me is to hoist twice and then rest for however long it takes, until I make it all the way to the top.

When I finally get there, I grab on to a branch, swing my leg up and over, and fall into a net that's woven between two branches with climbing rope—a dream catcher, they call it. I will never move again. Above me a tarp is stretched and tied to branches to help protect from weather. A tent in the trees. Woodruff climbs down from a branch to the platform below me. All I see are her climbing legs and her headlamp that glares at me whenever she looks my way. "You made it," she says.

"I don't really feel like I did," I say. I want to tell her about Peter, that I was too late, but she starts to explain what's what before I can. Here's some food. Here's a sleeping bag. Here's a pee jug. That's where you sleep. Try not to step on branches. You don't want to damage them. Do not, under any circumstance, ever, unhook from the ropes.

"This rope is life safe. It's what saves you from falling," she says, holding it so I can see. If you do fall, it's only about ten feet before finding the end of the rope and crashing into branches or the trunk, but, whatever. At least you're not dead. To move around the tree, you use two ropes attached to the harness that you then attach to different things, like branches or other ropes, so you're always attached in two different places for extra security. "I'm glad you're here," she says.

I kneel on my dream catcher to arrange the sleeping bag before climbing inside, which is complicated by all the ropes. Lying down is the best thing that has happened in weeks. I'm too tired to talk, but I have to know. "Are you worried about anyone on the ground tonight?"

"You never know, but I think we're cool," she says, sitting back and hanging in her harness. "They've done this before. They're just trying to see what we're doing and freak us out. You never know. I really should get back to Indigo," she says. I want to know what to do if they give us a hard time. They. God. It could be Nelson. Or, who knows? My dad. I don't really want to think about it. "Whatever you're comfortable with," she says. "You can just tell them you're not coming down until they guarantee the tree won't get cut and go limp if they come to get you." I ask about Justin. He's in a tree somewhere, too. He couldn't get back to camp either. "If it's safe on the ground tomorrow, he'll come by," she tells me, and then she climbs off to bed leaving me alone in the tree.

Everything aches—my muscles, my heart, my fingers. Now and then, the whole tree sways from side to side, and I sway with it and the branches wave gently in the wind. It's like being on a raft, only no water, a hundred feet above the ground. Drifting and floating in an ocean of redwoods. I pull the hood of the sleeping bag tight around my head and listen for the sound of mean, but I only hear the hoots of owls.

23

HALF AWAKE AND ASLEEP FOR hours in the early morning dark, dawn seems to stretch on forever. So many weird bits float through, pieces of dreams. I dream that golden web threads you can barely see run through everything. It is truly beautiful, but the thinnest most delicate threads are broken, floating unattached in the breeze. This is all I see. My arm is asleep for real, and I whack myself in the face by accident when I try to move it. I think: *When the blood gets cut off, you get pins and needles. You feel what's cut off wanting the blood to flow back.* And I know: When the golden threads are broken, it works the same way—what's cut off wants to be reattached. What we have now is lots of holes and floaty threads and everything wishing, dying, wanting to be attached again.

This is when I want to wake up, to understand what this means awake, not floating by on some dream. But the sway of the tree is so rock-a-bye, I stay somewhere in between awake and in dreams. With Everlast. I let myself flow into her. When I'm on the ground leaning back against a tree, what I get is trunk and roots. I fall back into it, let myself be what goes underground. But high in a tree and half asleep I don't get roots at all. This is different. What I get is branches and what's in between, breeze flowing, what reaches out, how it moves with so many other things, like another language.

If those golden threads really are real, let's give them something to do. I see threads run through the trunk and the branches, to the

144

neighbor trees and down into roots and to birds and through my heart, too. I see all of missing Peter begin to stretch from the fat, knot, ache that's balled-up in there, and I give it away, thinking, *Here. Take it. My sad.* And it flows from me blood red and stretches out like raindrops on a web. Everlast says, *Give it to me.* I keep giving it away because the tree and the threads feel that strong, broken web holes and all. Sad it can hold. Sad it can do something with. *Take it,* I think, *until it isn't red anymore, but gold.*

Deep inside the dark, cozy of my sleeping bag, I rest in the sweet of my dream, trying to absorb all of what it wants me to know. This happens sometimes. I'll be asleep and all of a sudden I see a picture that wants to tell me a story. It feels familiar, like something I've just said, except that when I try to wake to see it, it disappears. I don't get to know the dream at all, but the feeling stays with me, like I can still touch it. I always want to touch it.

Gliding on threads of gold in the growing morning light, chilly, fresh air sneaks in through a little hole where the sleeping bag hood is pulled tight. The tree pulls to one side, which could be the wind, but it's more of a quick pull than an easy flow. Sharp and quick jerks wake me for real.

Waking hurts. My muscles resist movement and I have to force myself to sitting. Raw, red blisters mark my fingers. Morning light and cool air are a shock, as is the fact that I'm in a tree on woven pea cord in between two branches. It really does look like one of those Native American webs that hangs above your bed to catch your dreams, only this dream catcher catches your entire body. One peek through the holes in the net and we're so high I can't even see the ground. Bad idea. Don't look down.

Two nearby trees have dream catchers, but no one is sleeping there. I'm alone with three huge redwoods. Traverse lines tied to Everlast go off to who knows where, tied to other trees with other kids and other platforms. A whole town in the treetops. A wood platform is situated below my net, two feet wide and five feet long, with buckets of food. Woodruff told me to help myself. "Commie food," she said, "as in, communal." She forgot that the only way I could help myself is if I climb down, which I do not plan on doing. She also showed me the pee bottle. Shit bucket is down below. I will not be visiting that either.

The tree pulls to one side again and someone is coming. The tug gets stronger the closer they get. The problem is that I can't do a damn thing about it because my body won't listen to anything I say. It's yelling at me. *I'm never moving again!* Branches thrash around where the traverse line is attached to the trunk. My heart races. They'll yell, *Come down from this tree!* I'll yell, *I can't!* They'll yell again, *You have to!* And I'll yell, *No, really. I really can't!* Ridiculous this not being able to move, stuck, waiting to get dragged down. But there is no yelling, no violent vibe. Just someone trying hard to get to Everlast. My dream floats off to somewhere else.

Someone is Justin pulling himself across the traverse line. He situates himself on a limb three branches above me and the sight of him is another whack my body can't take. Something inside of my chest turns into a knot. "Hey, Jade," he says. He said my name. He looks like he doesn't know if he's allowed to be here.

"Hey," I say. The sleeping bag is tangled at my feet.

"That climb was pretty rough, huh?" he says.

"Yeah," I say trying to rearrange myself. My harness is hitched up from the rope attached to a branch above me, which means my shirt is hitched too, squishy tummy flub saying hello to the world. I force myself to wrap the sleeping bag around me. My muscles are screaming, but screw it. He can't see my flub, too. I mean, really.

"You made it," he said.

"Barely," I say back, and we sit in the branches, the tree doing its side-to-side sway. Hunger rumbles around my stomach. Birds chitter nearby. He's waiting for me. After a long time, I finally talk. "You do not read someone's notebook, Justin. You just don't!"

Justin's eyes are fixed on me, unblinking and nervous. "I know," he says. "I'm sorry. I was wrong." His daddy longlegs dangle off the branch. The fact of us in a tree. He really is sorry.

"You really, really suck," I say.

"I know," he says, and he waits.

"Do you know about Peter?" I ask. Yes. "Do you know about Garden Lady?" Yes. "Do you know about 'just friends'?" Yes. "NO MERCY?" Yes. "Everything?" I ask.

"Mm-hmm," he says.

There's still a chance that he didn't find the secret pocket in the back of my notebook. I don't want to ask if he really does know everything about why I left.

"I was scared for you, man," he starts talking fast. "I thought you got, I don't know, raped or something. I didn't know. You were acting really weird, freaking back home and on the first day here and then you just disappeared."

"I didn't disappear," I tell him. "I went for a walk."

"Yeah," he says. "I didn't know that. And you know why?" He leans down from his branch and sticks his face toward me to make a point. "Because you didn't tell me." He straightens his upper body and stares me down for a minute, but then goes a little soft. "I wanted to help, but you weren't talking to me. I didn't know what to do because we're just friends. You know?" Yeah. "And that whole 'just friends' thing is bogus anyway." Nervousness keeps him talking. "I thought you only wanted to be just friends because you only wanted to hang. You never told me anything. Like where you're from, for example. Like you didn't want me to know you. So I thought I was just some boy toy."

Just some Justin. Still so yummy. Just still pissed. "You don't read people's notebooks, dude! You know everything! Who said I want you to?"

Guilt does strange things to a face. Justin's is drained of color. He looks down. "Well, it doesn't really matter, does it? Because how do I know that you're not always going to lie about what you're doing?" When he looks up, accusation hardens his eyes.

"I had good reasons for doing that," I say. I wasn't lying. I just couldn't tell him the truth.

"Well, so did I," he says. We're even. "I was worried about you. Don't you get that?" He wants me to get it. Someone worried about me. I was fine. "I get it," he said. "I messed up. I should have asked better." Our eyes lock in a standoff. No smiles, no giggles, just glaring each other down. Golden web threads so far away by now.

After a few minutes Justin's anger eases up and he breaks the silence. "So where'd you go yesterday?" It's just a question, but I get weird silent and start shaking my head. "What?" he says. I don't want them to, but the tears come. "What?" he says again. There are no words. It hurts to cry. He stands on his branch, hooks himself lower on the tree and climbs down to sit on my holey net. He crawls onto the dream catcher and wraps himself around me. Through the holes it's so far down. "You've got to tell me about these tears, Jade."

"Peter's gone." The words are more of a choke than a whisper. "I didn't stop it." Tears flow down my checks. He holds me. I make a sniffly mess of his flannel shirt and I cry until I can't cry anymore. Some of my mad leaves, too. He knows what it means.

Tree time is its own time, and you lose yourself in it. We cuddle under my sleeping bag on the dream catcher that gets narrow like a piece of pie where the branches meet the trunk. It's tight, but cozy. I tell him about my day—Skatio for sale, my walk along the Eel River, the salmon, the clear-cut, no Peter, how Grey Goose found me. He listens and then we steep in silence.

"I don't think you're that weird talking to Peter," he finally says. "I think most people talk to something. They just don't admit it, even to themselves." I wonder if that's true. "I talk to Granny Gertie all the time," he says about his grandmother I've never heard about. Granny Gertie is dead, smoked a pipe and made lots of pies with Justin when he was a kid in Minnesota.

"Minnesota, huh?" My fingers twirl in his wavy hair. "I didn't know that."

"You didn't ask," he says, and he turns and gives me such an eat-me kiss. "There's a lot to get to know now, isn't there?" he says.

Oh yes. Yes there is, lying on a net, in a tree, making out. "One small problem," I say.

"And what is that?" he says into my mouth, kissing.

"I can't move," I remind him. "And everything hurts."

"Well that's true," he says between kisses. "But your mouth works!"

That's true too, but kissing when you're so sad is kind of like making yourself eat when you're not hungry—you just don't want things in your mouth. Plus every now and then my brain says *A hundred feet high!* for no good reason. Turns out that sad and so sore and tree sitting don't mix for making out. At least not in me, not right now. "It's just this height thing." I can barely talk about it without getting goofy in my belly.

"Okay," he says. "If I have to wait, I'll snack on you later, but only if you promise." I promise with as much kiss as I can manage. We settle into a cozy cuddle, each of us in our harnesses, tangled in ropes, trying to stay warm under my sleeping bag.

Justin tells me how his day went down. He went to the tree sit with Grey Goose, Woodruff, Daisy, and Spore and all the goods. He made the climb to see what it was like and loved it. They're hanging out in a group of trees they call the Triad when Grey Goose hears something. A few minutes later they see this guy in a hard hat walking around below them. They call down to him, but he doesn't say anything. He's walking to different trees, looking to the branches, scanning the canopy. "He was so clearly trying to get a read on the scene," he says. "It was totally freaky."

I want to know what the guy looked like. I don't want to ask.

He was there for half an hour when another guy came. Grey Goose kept yelling down to them things like, "How you doing today? I hope you're not picking which trees to fall here. There are people living in these trees, you know!" They ignored him. Just walked around taking notes. Grey Goose told everyone they'd have to stay for the night. "It's pretty sketch," he told them. "Being arrested is almost guaranteed if you're on the ground. We're safe here for now."

It wasn't too long after the guys left that they heard someone yelling, "No! No!" Peter isn't that far from the tree sit, I guess. Close enough to hear yelling. Grey Goose risked it, climbed down to see if someone was hurt, and found me.

Justin's story reminds me that we are not camping. This is not a relaxing few days floating in a dream catcher. We're sitting in the last trees left in the area to save them. Sitting where we're not allowed to be, where loggers like Nelson want to drag us down. I should be scared, really scared, actually. But I don't have it in me. It's too much work. There is only resting, feeling the way the breeze and the trees move. And Justin, too, how he moves and smells and tastes. Everything else feels so far away. What has happened. What could happen.

Justin bolts upright. "We need to eat! I need food!" I remind him I can't move. "I've got you covered," he says, and he untangles himself from me and the ropes and crawls from the sleeping bag. He climbs down to the commie platform and digs through the buckets. He finds a book. "Here, read this!" he throws me a book about trees that I slide into the bottom of my sleeping bag for later. Justin fishes ramen noodles from the bucket. He starts the camp stove, cooks them, and manages to climb back to the dream catcher with the pot. We eat. We slurp. It's true. These are the best ramen noodles I have ever eaten. A bag of chocolate chips magically appears from the back pocket of his baggy pants. He eats them only one at a time. "I want to learn to savor everything," he says, his eyes closed, yumming on a single chocolate chip. I try it, too. Chocolate chips rock, but one at a time is nowhere near enough. I don't really feel like more.

"So what are you going to do?" Justin breaks the savoring silence. He's only asking. He pulls another chocolate chip from of the bag and places it in his mouth.

"About what?" I say, sounding easy-going, but I know what he means. Trying to not think about it.

"Are you staying here?" Ropes stretch from Everlast to kids lying in their own little nets in the tree village. All of us swaying in the treetops.

"I don't know," I say turning pieces of my life over in my mind—my sweet little replants all wilted back in Portland; Garden Lady doing her thing and me doing it with her; Lily; the clear-cut where Peter's gone; Liza like Batman without her Robin; what can happen when no one stands in the way of too much logging; and, also, what happens when they do. "I don't know," I say again. "Are you?"

151

"Absolutely." He doesn't miss a beat. As if it were as simple as that.

Even in the branches I feel the solid strength of Everlast standing right here for six-hundred-something years, surviving everything that has come her way. I lie on that, warm and safe for now, swaying in the tangle of it all. Funny how the things that you worry will happen usually don't, but what you don't expect to happen can wreck your world.

"Have you told anyone?" he asks.

"Tell who what?" I play dumb. I know what he means again. He won't drop it.

He takes a minute before he answers, waiting for the last of his chocolate chip to dissolve. "You've been around town. People could have seen you. It could be why they were here. Did you think of that? They could be looking for you."

I've thought of it. "Why would they come here?" I say.

"Ummm, because you're missing," he says like it's obvious.

"No one saw me," I say. "Besides, they'd be here anyway when kids are in the trees. They know everything that goes on here. I have nothing to do with it." A rush of wind flows through the treetops, and the dream catcher branches wave gently up and then down.

"What about that guy in the truck?" A bit of Jeremiad in Justin's voice now, a hard edge to it.

"No one saw me, okay? He was just some guy."

"Yeah, some guy who knew everything about Skatio and could know everything about you, too."

Ed didn't know it was me. Or if he did, he wasn't letting on. "I just don't know why they'd come here looking for me, that's all. I could be anywhere."

Justin pulls his arm from under my head, sits up, and looks at me like I'm a dope. "What is your problem?" he says. "You know, I don't really care why those guys were here yesterday. I just don't want them around. And if you being here makes it dangerous for the rest of us, then I think it's only fair to let people know."

There is nothing to say to this. Justin and what he knows, his school-of-life, know-it-all crap. Making it about me. Endless branches twitch around, and the tarp crinkles in the wind.

Justin and all of his limbs are quick to leave the sleeping bag. "Where are you going?" I ask. He doesn't answer. Whatever love fest was happening between us is now gone. Just like that. "Grey Goose knows I'm from here, okay?"

"Yeah, but does he know you *ran away* from here?" Justin squats on the dream catcher, looks at me, and then stares straight ahead and waits for my answer. I don't say a word. No one can know what went down. Speaking it makes it real. I'm not even supposed to be here now. I keep trying to leave and yet here I am. Not ready. Justin climbs to a branch and yanks on ropes, trying to see which ones are his because we're tangled. "It was freaky when those dudes were here, all right? I saw them. You don't even know how scary it was." He stops to look at me. "Or do you? Actually, I don't really know what you know." His juicy lips form a tight line, his green eyes are round. All he sees is sides. I've seen that look in the eyes of the guys on the porch at The What Not. Us against Them.

"Look, Justin. You sitting in these trees is not going to change things much. *That* I know." That look never wins anything. Both sides are right and both sides are wrong and nobody actually listens. "You might save a tree or maybe two, but they always find a new place to cut." He stares at me like he can't believe what I just said. I can't believe what I said, either. "People always want more. Don't you get that?" None of this is what I want to say.

"That's a good one, coming from you." Justin untangles the

last of his rope and clips himself into the traverse line by his head. I'm the bad guy now. Maybe it's true.

"This isn't some game you play for just a little while, you know. Just when you feel like it!" I'm on my knees now. I don't know how this happens. "I thought you weren't even an activist! You said we were going camping and now you're some tree-sit hero?" I want to pull it all back in my mouth.

"Whatever," he says, and he falls back into the branches. The weight of his body swings him out across the rope. He pulls himself away from me, hand over hand, the tug of his movements growing less and less as he disappears into the sea of needles.

All I want is to be asleep. I fall back into my dream catcher, close my eyes to make the day go away, and let myself drift in the giant net of this pack of kids camped in the canopy of hundreds of years of being here, steeping in all of that with birds and squirrels and salamanders and owls and millions of other crawly things that live here, too. But then I see how if one of the trees goes down, we all go down with it. How we're all tied together. I drift on that, too. Drifting bigger than anything now. What could happen like some fly buzzing around my head.

24

IT IS STILL DAY WHEN I OPEN my eyes again. The forest is quiet except for far-off birds and the wind that seems to be moving more swiftly through the branches. Leaning on my forearms to save the blisters on my fingers, I inchworm out of the sleeping bag. Time to eat and to not be lame. The commie platform is two branches below with buckets of food.

I unhook one of the two ropes on my harness from where it is wrapped around the branch above me, crawl a few feet, and hook it to a rope that's tied around the trunk. This is when I notice that my second rope is attached way back at the other end of the dream catcher. When I go back to unhook that, there isn't enough line from my rope at the trunk to make it all the way. The blue rope hangs just out of reach. My muscles are crying. They want to be in a permanent fetal position, not crawling around some tree, but I turtle-crawl my sorry butt back to the trunk anyway and unhook from there. Repeat the whole exercise, leapfrogging the ropes, making sure to give myself enough slack.

Wind whistles through branches and the day is not turning blue, but stays gray.

At the trunk, I don't want to step on branches and the only option for getting down to the platform is to lower myself. Pray the ropes are connected right, sit back in my harness and even though I swing, it holds. Three elephants. Life safe. Time to let go. The rope slides across the raw of my hands as I rappel and a deep, quick breath in stifles a yell from the pain as I yank the rope to stop my fall. Slide an elbow over a nearby branch that offers a place to rest and talk myself into dropping some more. Food and peeing are my only motivation. I have to poop, but that's not going to happen. It's not because I'm too pansy for the shit bucket. It just doesn't seem like a very good idea right now.

My feet finally touch the platform and standing on something like a floor feels so ridiculously good that I laugh out loud. The platform is tiny, half the size of a twin bed. Commie buckets filled with food, matches, cooking utensils and the camp stove take most of the space and bigger items like jugs of water, cooking oil and pans hang from ropes tied around the tree. There's little room to move, but I find my place.

Making a meal makes me incredibly proud and feels so normal—grabbing a pan filling it with water, using matches to light the stove. But then I look over the side to way down there, and my whole body feels like it's falling. Everlast takes a long, slow sway. Three elephants is a load of crap when you get a full-body freak. I scoot my butt away from the edge of the platform, take a deep breath and fill my lungs until there is no room left in them anymore, hold it and count to ten. Breathe out slow. I do this over and over.

What the hell am I doing cooking in a tree?

The meal loses its appeal and my dream catcher feels like the safest place in the world. Apples and peanut butter from the commie bucket will be good enough. I shove them in a plastic bag, turn off the camp stove, and ditch the water from the pan over the side. The sound of water falling undoes my brain—how far to the ground? How much hits the branches? How much falls in between? "Stop it," I say aloud as if I'm talking to someone besides myself.

Everything happens in reverse. Holding on to my bag of food, I stand in the stirrup, slide my chest knot up, lean back in my harness, slide my foot knot up, grab the rope, step into the stirrup again, and hoist my whole body. A blister tears, and pain shoots across my hand. I do it again. Nerves in my bones make me do it. Climbing is not falling.

My dream catcher is heaven, but there is nowhere to put anything down because nets have holes and branches are round. It's a game of one thing at a time. Sitting on my net, I lay the plastic bag on the sleeping bag, remove the apple and the peanut butter and lay them on top. Remove the lid from the peanut butter and, because I'm thirsty, lean to grab the water bottle that's tied to the branch. Everything tilts. The peanut butter tips over, and my apple rolls off the sleeping bag and falls through a hole in the net. The sound of the apple falling. Screw it. My finger wipes the nut butter that oozed onto the sleeping bag and I lick it off. I drink my water. My finger becomes an eating utensil that scoops globs from the jar that I then stick in my mouth. I drink more water. I have to pee. Now's the time, because I really have to go and because when I finally lie back down, I will never move again.

The lid screws back on the peanut butter which I shove back in the plastic bag and shove the plastic bag into my backpack, which is jammed into the dream catcher where the branch meets the tree. The pee jug tied at the far end of the dream catcher is nasty—a big water jug with pee inside and a funnel tied at the neck. The impossible challenge is to shimmy your pants from under the harness while holding the funnel in the jug and get busy standing over it. But how do you stand over it on a net? And how do you pee without getting it all over yourself? You can't. Instead I kneel and try to slide my harness and my pants down to my knees, which means that I'm not really roped in. Stupid crazy. Who knows who can see me. I try again, kneeling over the stinky funnel and the jug, tangled in my ropes, peeing, saying,

"Don't panic, don't panic. I'm only peeing."

What the hell am I doing peeing in a tree?

Yeah. Pooping. I am not doing that.

Screw the top back on the pee-jug nastiness and let it drop on its rope off the side of the branch. Shimmy my pants and harness back to where they're meant to be. Find the opening to my sleeping bag that smells like peanut butter and slide down into it, my ropes connected to where they're still tied above me. I curl into myself deep inside, where it's dark and warm, where I am no longer Mazzy Jazzy Jade or whatever my name is, stuck in a grove. I am no one at all and the puff of the sleeping bag blocks the sound of the wind.

25

GETTING IN TO SEE PETER is never easy. The hike isn't
hard, even though it is a little far from home. There is the weird
tangle of roots wrapped around slick rocks, wrapped around
other roots and huge trees with spongy bark all in a circle. Furry,
moist moss stretches over the rocks and roots in places. You have
to be careful of slipping or catching your ankle in a hole. It can
take time.

And there is Lily. Everything takes longer with Lily. We
pack little snacks of our favorite things. I try not to ask her what
she wants because she'll say, "Well what is there?" No matter
what I tell her we have, she says, "Uuummmm . . . no. I don't
want that. What else do we have?" We'd be there all day. So I
stopped asking her and now only pack crackers and salami and
peppermint candies. We always have a huge bag of peppermints.
Dad likes them in his lunch.

We never walk in a straight line. Lily beelines for a flower or
a rock. It doesn't matter, because she collects everything. Stringy,
green lichen (witch's hair!), acorns (fairy chairs!), rocks of all sizes
(monster vitamins!). I have to carry whatever she collects because
she'll whine if I don't and tell me that she'll tell Santa not to
bring me anything if I don't carry it for her. One day I finally
told her we were on a secret mission just to get her moving. Her
round eyes got wide. "Really?" That worked.

We made our way into the Circle of Giants after a slow and
careful climb, helping each other across the tricky spots. It felt

like we'd crossed some invisible wall, and we fell back on the needles with our knees bent and our backpacks under our heads. Streams of light snuck in between the branches, and we watched the bazillion floaty things float around in the air that you never really see unless you're looking for them. We wondered how high it would be before you'd see the sky and if ants feel the same way when they look toward the tip of a blade of grass.

Lying inside the circle, stepping into forever, there is no us and them. There is no right or wrong. There is only good, deep quiet and the things we do trying to remember how to get back inside that stillness.

I'd tell Lily the things I saw, just to keep her quiet—a man sitting cross-legged under a tree, how there are so many shapes in what is invisible, a current you can ride like a roller coaster across circles that dip and rise and curve into other shapes, a group of people looking at a bird soaring above them, what noise looks like. Sometimes, people fighting on a field, like war.

Lily loved this. She'd sit so quiet and wait. "Tell me more!" She'd almost yell if I didn't speak for a while. "Tell me more mobile stories!" She had a mobile above her bed at home, and when I told her these little stories, she pictured them on some mobile in her head and watched them float around there. I never told her the heavy stuff. Only the sweet things, like soaring birds. For fun, I told her that smells and sounds were included, too. "Even Gramps's smelly farts?" she asked, and she scrunched her nose.

"Even those," I said.

I was dumb and taught her how to make spit bubbles from the spit in your mouth. You roll them around under your tongue until you get a good one that sits on the top of your tongue and then blow it off so it floats in the air without popping. It's hard to do, but Lily got good at it. If I was too quiet for too long, she'd start letting the spit bubbles fly. Sometimes, they weren't bubbles at all, but spitty splootches.

One landed on my cheek one day. I opened my eyes, and she was leaning over my face, her brow furrowed. "Are you good weird or weird weird?" she asked, trying to decide which weird I was. I'd been far away for some time, I guess, seeing people go at each other, fighting old-school, weapons in hand, on a field. Vicious mad was bigger than everyone, one side against the other. Some fight with no real reason, no reason they could remember anyway. Somehow I stood in the middle of it, knowing that no one knew why they were fighting anymore. Empty and attacking. A sound seemed to rise above the clash. I turned toward it, straining to hear, but as I did, the sound was suddenly not a sound, but a feeling deep in my chest, invisible and bigger than everything around me. Love. As simple as that. Looking for a place to land.

That's when the spit bubble plonked on my cheek. Lily and her chubby, round face, her dotty freckles and bright brown eyes looking to see what was taking me so long. She watched me for a minute. "Weird weird," she decided, and she sat back down.

Forever always calls to me, reminding me what's there. What you can feel and hear even in the middle of so much noise. What's in your heart and how you can give it away, like trees give away air, because nothing works if there is only taking. *Everything that connects me to you, Peter, connects me to forever. A trail leads me there.* Deep inside the dark of my sleeping bag, I try to catch every little bit. Hold on to it all.

I only want to be in forever.

Live in what will outlive you.

Are you there now?

26

HOOTS AND MONKEY SOUNDS make it through the fluff of my bag. I poke my head out of the stuffy dark, and the new day is so fresh. I've slept for that long. The cold wakes the inside of my nose and fills my lungs down deep. Grey Goose is yelling, "Breakfast at Everlast!"

My turtle crawl is not as bad as it was, but it's not that good either. My blisters are there, but not quite so sore. I make it to my backpack at the end of the dream catcher near the tree and drag it back to my spot on the net. Everlast feels tugs from all directions as elephant spiders start to appear one by one. Daisy and Grey Goose arrange themselves on the platform. Justin ropes in to a branch, hangs in his harness, and doesn't look at me. Woodruff climbs in from the same direction he did and finds a place to hang from her harness, too. Spore sits on one of the branches of my dream catcher. "Great to see you, Jazzy!" they say. "Cool you're here!"

"Yeah, it's good to be here," I say because it actually is. So nice to see everyone. The day is chilly and foggy and very still. I'm feeling a little stronger. I grab my journal from my backpack. I don't want to lose the forever bits floating by on some dream. Grey Goose and Daisy are the camp cooks and get busy with eggs and coffee, and the smell of it mixes with the fresh air. I could kiss them for making breakfast.

Spore knocks into my backpack and sees the peanut butter. "Dude!" he says slow. "Get this away from me." He pulls his arms and legs into his body and leans back against the trunk. "Keep it away! I'm allergic."

"Well, send it here!" Justin says. "I love peanut butter!" Spore keeps his distance from the tub as I pass the peanut butter to Justin, who doesn't bother to acknowledge my existence. Moody jerk. His curly brown-gold hair looks scruffy, bed head, mashed on one side. He snaps the tub from my hands and holds it like it's gold. "Oh my god, I love peanut butter!" He opens it, rests it in his lap, and digs in with his finger.

"You know what I love?" Daisy says. "I love rice bread." She kneels on the platform bundled in layers of jackets, holding a full coffee filter over the rim of a cup with one hand and pouring hot water over it with the other. Her floppy Mohawk is punk-rock, but it's also longish and girl-cute.

"You know what I love?" Justin talks with peanut butter stuck in his mouth. "Any gluten-free bread. I'm allergic to everything else."

Grey Goose kneels on the platform and scrambles eggs in a fry pan on the camp stove. "You know what I love? I love you, dude!" he says, and he points the eggy spatula at Justin.

Justin stops chewing. "Awww. You're so sweet," he says like he's talking to a kitten. Justin or not, it feels like a happy, goofy breeze has just blown into Everlast. Just what I need. I write in my journal:

Air that I breathe.
Roots beneath your feet hold everything together.
Home to so many things.

Spore adds his two cents in his quiet way. "Sunflower butter is the best anyway."

"Oh, man, that is rank! Cashew butter is the best!" Grey Goose says.

Daisy pulls the coffee filter from one cup and plops it into another. "Since when did everyone get allergic to everything?"

Justin turns into Jeremiad. "Since the industrial-food complex kicked into high gear and separated the people from the land and started making everything for us with fake crap." This makes him think of something. "What kind of oil do you cook with anyway?"

I write:

Live in what will outlive you.

Grey Goose hands Justin a cup of coffee, which he trades for the peanut butter. "Coconut oil, usually. Is there any here, Woodruff? I left mine back on the platform in Shazam." His tree, I guess.

"What's the story on coconut oil?" Spore asks.

Spider Justin hangs in his harness without holding on, his hands wrapped around his coffee, the steam whisping into the morning air. "Most oils break down when they get heated, but you can heat coconut oil to like four hundred degrees or something before it breaks down. It's super good for you." This could be an infomercial. Or a cooking show.

What Justin told me on our walk pops into my head. I write that down, too:

Shinrin yoku: a walk in the woods is a bath for your soul.

Grey Goose passes another coffee to Justin, who passes it to Spore, who passes it to me. I drop my journal in my lap and take it. Hot coffee is better than heaven. Talk skips around and goes from homemade kombucha tea to how to ferment to what internal cleanse works best, some super paprika cleanse that takes all the toxins and makes your lymph nodes swell. Steamy coffee is hot electricity running through my body.

Daisy changes the topic. "Anyone have recurring dreams?" she asks, making her last cup of coffee.

Back in the land of the living and feeling mighty perky, I tell them all about my weird tree-of-light dream, the one where I have to name the light but can never remember the name. "I'm always about to name it when I wake up," I say. "I hate when the dream starts because I know that I'm going to forget it. All I want is to know the name of the damn light and see what happens when I say it. Makes me nuts."

Spore sips on his coffee and says in his slow, windy way, "I don't know if you're supposed to name anything." His input is like a flat tire, not a whole lot of help.

"I don't know," I say. "The whole dream is about what to name it."

"No. I'm serious," he says. "Have you ever looked at yourself standing there in the dream?" And it's true, I haven't. Suddenly I want to be asleep again, see what's coming from me standing there.

"He's really good at dreams." Daisy sits on her feet that are crossed under her. She digs in to her eggs. There's so much kind in her big sweet eyes. How much she loves what Spore says comes over me like a wave.

Spore leans back against the trunk and looks over the grove. Fog is thick as oatmeal, and there is not too much to see other than damp gray. "I just think we've forgotten how to read signs, you know, what's in our dreams. Things we see around us. It's like some ancient way of knowing the world that's been lost." He sips his coffee. "Native people almost everywhere have always believed more in dreams than what we see around us. It's like the awake world is where we work things out, where we get to make choices. The dream world is where we get to know what the possibilities are." He says this so la-di-da, like he's talking about the weather. "I just have fun trying to decipher the code." All this from the gentlest, sweetest anarchist that barely ever talks. I want to ask him a million things. Like love on a battlefield. What do you do with that?

"How old are these trees around here?" Justin changes the topic.

"There are a few really old, old-growth trees in the area, like Everlast," Grey Goose says. I feel her with us tiny elephant spiders, hanging midair in her branches. No ground in sight. "But mostly it's second growth." He sits back on his butt, carefully pulls his feet from under him, and wraps his arms around his knees. "Since there's been logging there has also been some planting. This area was cut around 1900 and then planted, so these trees are around one hundred years old. That's why this grove is so important to save. All the oldest trees are in parks, but these second-oldest trees aren't protected. If this goes, the wildlife that needs these woods has nowhere to go. The water in the creeks that run through here won't be clean anymore." The plan is to build some kind of mall close by, and they want to clear the woods around it, too, for who knows why. Selling all the logs, maybe. All for a mall with its stuff and food courts. "If they were smart about it, they could thin the forest and move some of the wood and still keep this land healthy at least. No need to do away with it completely."

"I don't know about that," Woodruff breaks into the conversation after hanging quietly with her feet propped on a branch. I'd forgotten she was there. "Forget even thinning. I think we should leave everything alone and let the earth heal itself. We've done enough damage. Don't you think?" She directs this question at Grey Goose and doesn't even blink. She always says exactly what she thinks.

"Well, if this grove was taken care of it could become a healthy old-growth forest one day and, in the meantime, keep the local economy limping along a little," he says. "There has to be some kind of logging. Forests just can't be completely left alone."

Woodruff rolls her eyes. "Forests have survived for millions of years without us. No reason they really need us now."

"I don't know about that." Grey Goose pulls on the straggly threads on the ends of his ratty pants. His feet are filthy. "One way we can help with all the damage is to keep what forests we have left healthy. We can thin them, cut just some of the trees so wildfires aren't so bad, for one thing . . ."

Woodruff interrupts. "Well, I think the problem is that we assume we know what the right thing is. Who are we to know what to do with what's lived for a thousand years? Humans suck, as far I'm concerned. We think we know so much. Maybe we should try to learn something instead."

Grey Goose laughs and looks at me and then Spore. "We do this all the time," he says, as if he has to explain the argumentative tone. They've known each other forever, traveling from tree sit to tree sit and other places, trying to save what they don't want to see hurt. They take a few breaks and do training workshops in between.

Woodruff kind of laughs but is clearly annoyed, and plays with the end of her dreads. "Yeah. We don't really agree on this topic."

Silence settles over us as we sit and eat in the drifty branches and billions of needles. Even Justin is quiet, which I can't believe because this is just his kind of talk. Unless, of course, he's actually listening, realizing he's way out of his league. He makes himself hang upside down, and he really does look like a spider with his knees bent and his feet on the rope. Wind blasts through in short gusts and nudges branches that wave around a little more than I'd like. No one else seems to notice. I pass my empty coffee cup to Spore, who nestles it in his cup and then plunks them down on top of my backpack.

The list of sayings in my journal looks imprisoned living only on the page, so I set it free. I tear out each dream float, little paper rectangles, one by one, and lay them in a pile on my lap. Twine is in the commie bucket on the platform. Daisy throws it to me when I ask.

Grey Goose breaks the silence. "I don't think you're being very realistic, Woodruff," he says. "Logging can't really go away, because if you stop all logging, you're also making whole towns go down the drain. That means people's livelihoods. Whole communities."

"Jade knows something about that, don't you, Jade?" Justin says. Hearing my name in a tree. I almost don't know who he's talking about at first, and then I feel on the spot. He looks at me, daring me.

"Who's Jade?" Daisy asks.

"She is." Justin points my way.

All faces on me now. "Long story," I say. "I changed my name. Again."

Woodruff could care less. She isn't done with Grey Goose. "Look, I think if we can find a way to send a man to the moon, we can find a way for a community to learn a new set of skills." I'm off the hook, for now.

"All I'm saying is I think there's a way to do what's healthy for the forest and the communities. It may take more time and be more expensive than clear-cutting, but . . ."

Woodruff doesn't wait for him to finish. "There is no compromise anymore!" The volume of her voice doubles as she holds on to her rope and leans toward him. "We're too far gone. It's time to stop, and if you believe otherwise, you're eating all the crap they're feeding you. We're sick. Don't you get that? Addicted to more. There is nothing reasonable about that and there's no choice but to try to stop it. At any cost!"

Grey Goose doesn't back down and he talks louder, too. "There are ways to thin forests that can still keep an economy going and keep a forest healthy. We need wood, don't we? It's just all this mass cutting with no respect for the health of the land that has wrecked everything so bad."

Woodruff gets in the last word. "Anyway," she says, and she throws her hair over her shoulder and looks over the grove, which is all swaying now. I wish it would stop. She braids her dreads together. Grey Goose laughs and looks away. Woodruff takes a big breath in and doesn't let it go. All of us tree-sit virgins don't know what to say, so no one says anything.

I take the tag with the first thing I ever learned from Peter written on it, poke a hole in the end of the paper with my pen, grab a pocket knife from my backpack, cut a piece of twine, and thread it through. I tie the tag to a small nearby branch. *Nothing works if there is only taking* flutters in the wind, and a huge rush fills the whole of me, as if what jumped from Peter down in his roots spread to the roots next door and then the roots next door to that like some happy virus that eventually found its way to me. The Here It Comes comes on strong, and I let it flow in to me and through me. Right here, right now. Spore grabs the tip of the tree tag between his fingers, enough to hold it still while he reads. A big smile spreads across his face.

"What do you think about all this, Jade?" Justin is on a roll.

I know what he's doing. "I think I'm tired of impossible situations," I say, and I poke around my pile of tags, trying to decide which one will be next. "And I think I'm tired of everyone losing and nobody winning." Which is true. I'll say what I want when I'm ready.

"Well, I'm with Woodruff," Jeremiad says, talking fast now,

dead serious, a rant just dying to get going. "There is no compromise anymore. I think we should do something more than just sit here, something that actually shuts them down. Whatever it takes. I don't think the mill is that far from here."

"Whoa, whoa, whoa," Grey Goose stands on the platform and talks directly to Justin now. "Dude, you have got to pipe down. What are you talking about?" Justin doesn't look at him but looks nervous at Woodruff, who looks at her pants. The vibe gone from sweet to sour as quick as the wind starts to blow harder.

I know what he's talking about. Ways to put companies out of business—blow things up or damage property to slow the workflow or make them lose tons of money, or hurt someone enough to scare them into stopping. Actions that keep the fighting going. "If you do anything like you're thinking, Justin, you're no different than them," I say quietly. Tension sits in the trees with us now. Justin looks at me for a minute like he's going to say something, but doesn't. Wishing the wind and what's unsaid would leave us all alone.

"This is not some game, dude." Grey Goose is normally so cool, but this he yells, not hiding his mad anymore. "We've been carrying this grove for months. We're making our point. We don't mess with their crap. If you want to deal in that bs, you can find other kids to do it with. Got it?"

Justin doesn't say anything but fiddles with the end of one of his ropes. After a minute he says under his breath, "As long as you think we're making our point."

A gust comes up quick, and Everlast sways too far to one side. "Whoa. What's with the weather?" I ask. Everyone holds on to something like we're on a boat in a choppy sea.

"Oh, it's just a little wind," Woodruff says like I'm a wimp, even though she has to yell a little to make herself heard. She hangs in her harness, swaying with the rest of us, not holding on to anything as she sighs and sips the last of her coffee. "Probably a few sprinkles."

Just a little wind is getting under my skin. Everyone keeps quiet to see which way this conversation will go. Everlast sways back to center again. Grey Goose lets go of his rope and rearranges things on the commie platform, like nothing is organized right. No one knows what to say. Justin shoots looks at Woodruff, who doesn't look back at him and doesn't talk anymore, either. The end of the conversation, at least for now.

Spore finally takes a harmonica from his pocket, sucks in and starts to play a sweet thread of a sound that mingles with the wet and wild of the forest. Daisy adds her voice, and they play tag, wandering through harmonies, crossing over each other sometimes and landing on top of each other, too. Their tune untangles my nerves from the knot they're in, just a bit. The little pile of tree tags sits in my lap. Tree dreams no longer only in me, but not attached anywhere in the world yet either. I make a cup with my hands and cover them over so they don't blow away.

We listen to the music, blown about in our own little world one hundred feet high, trying to decide what comes next. Worried, wondering, and at the same time just making up songs, crushing on each other, fighting, loving peanut butter and chocolate chips. It is what it is. What we have now.

"Well, on that note," Woodruff finally says, itchy to get on with the day. She reminds us that it's Saturday, which means that anyone who wants to climb down has to be ready in a few hours. It should be safe. She has to go in to town, and she'll take anyone back to camp who wants to go, but no one does. Everyone plans to stay at the tree sit, a little unhappy with each other now. In the meantime, it's time for chores. Spore will head off to help Grey Goose weave a new dream catcher, Daisy will sew a ripped tarp, and Justin will be with Woodruff for some reason that's not very clear.

"What's your story, Maz?" Woodruff asks, still hanging in her harness. I can't tell if she only wants to know whether I'm staying or if Justin has said something to her about me and she's digging for info. Justin's already on a traverse line, but going slowly like he's waiting for Woodruff.

I sit in my dream catcher, like some fish on dry land, my hands cupped over the pile of tree tags in my lap. The nonstop wind will not let up. "Can I tell you soon?" I ask. "I have something to do first." My plan is taking shape as I speak. Justin pretends to not be interested and pulls himself away on the traverse. "I might stay," I say loud enough because maybe I will. I can't tell if he heard me.

"Awesome," she says, as if I had said yes, and she unhooks her ropes from the tree and hooks herself into the traverse line. "You can help me with the shit buckets."

"Great," I say, like I can handle it. Shit buckets. I've got to decide.

Woodruff falls back and starts to pull herself away, too. "I'll come get you in an hour or so," she yells, and she climbs off in the same direction as Justin.

27

ALONE WITH EVERLAST AND THE whoosh of the wind, I grab my journal and lay it on top of the tags in my lap so they don't blow away. I write one more:

> *Trees communicate through their roots.*
> *Messages are sent right under our feet through what*
> *we think is 'just dirt.' This is how life moves on.*

I cut this tag and add it to my pile. One by one I poke little holes in the paper with my pen, cut enough twine, and thread the brown string through. Dream floats on torn paper rectangles ready to go.

A picture flashes in my mind: tree dreams tied on branches in a Family Circle around Skatio so that this up-for-sale town can know the dreams of trees, too, remember at least some of what we have somehow forgotten and write a new story of what comes next. I'll tie them here in the woods, on a tree at the market, in front of the mill, at the school, at the post office, on a branch of the old eucalyptus at the bend in the Eel, by the pharmacy, at the hotel. In front of my house. In front of Liza's. In front of Nelson's.

This is what I will do.

Coffee and scrambled eggs have changed my world. Sliding from my sleeping bag and on to my knees is not so hard now. It's only a little weather making everything move. Woodruff said so. Nothing but a few sprinkles. I'm tied into Everlast, and my ropes are life safe. The plastic bag from my fallen apple is still jammed in my backpack, perfect for tree tags. I shove them in, put the pack on my back, and shove everything else I don't need down into the bottom of my sleeping bag. I stand, for real, for the first time in two whole days. Leg muscles remind me of this, taking time to be long.

There are so many ways out of Everlast. The dream catcher is woven ropes and holes in between. I step where it holds me, one step at a time, feeling my way. Don't look down. Unhook the rope from the branch overhead, step forward, and hook myself to the rope at the trunk, wobble back, unhook my second rope, and make it back to the trunk. I attach that rope to a traverse line that heads off at two o'clock from Everlast. No one has come or gone this way that I have seen. I clip in even though I don't know where it goes. I don't listen to the wind. Branches twitch angry now, and gray is getting darker, but here I am. Woodruff could be wrong. Me, my ropes, my harness, and my plastic bag of tree dreams. I take a deep breath and fall back. The little oval metal piece attached to the end of my rope slides onto the traverse line, and I slide out with it.

First I fall and then swing back and forth, hanging on my rope, my legs dangling from the seat of my harness. My second rope is still attached to the trunk and I pull myself back to Everlast, which is as wide as a wall. No way to wrap my arms around her. I unhook myself and attach that rope to my harness. This is really happening. Don't look down. Hanging now from only the traverse line overhead, I pull myself away, everything flowing a little easier now, hand over hand, feeling so rad. *Look at how brave I am!* The rain spitting little bits.

The more I pull, the farther I get to in between. The traverse rope droops down from the weight of me, the other end attached to I don't know where. I stop, pull myself to sitting, lean forward against the rope, close my eyes, put my hand in the plastic bag, and grab a tag.

Roots beneath your feet hold everything together.

I shove the bag down and hold it between my knees. Random rain pelts the plastic, the rest of the weather caught by millions of needles. This is not smart. Everything twitching now. Nothing but branches. I grab one and hold on to the end of it, steadying its sway, and tie the tag on tight. The sound of my breathing, heavy from the climb, mixed with the wind, my breath showing itself in cold air. Raindrops fall on my face and lips. I lick them off. Traversing people will now see magic when they cross. Here It Comes full flow in me now, a smile on my lips. *Here it is, Peter, from you to me to the world to see.*

My fingers are cold and wet from what is not a storm. They are stiff, but there is more to do. I pull myself along the rope in midair, quicker now. Stop. Sit. Pick another tag. The thrash of the trees is getting on my nerves. When will it stop?

Live in what will outlive you.

I tie it on. Branches whip around. The rope I'm hanging on swings from side to side. The traverse line moves, too, back and forth like the trees are playing tug of war and I'm the flag in the middle. *This isn't just a little weather.* And then everything sways more to one side than it has yet. I feel it in my bones, the storm that's not coming, that's already here.

Branches part above me, and a mad batch of black knotty clouds are overhead. A giant wind rolls like a wave on the sea of needles that all of a sudden look blue green where the branches are bent backward. *This is not good.* They twist and bend like silly little ropes in the wind. Tree dreams hold on, flipping and twirling around. Rain comes in sideways. I hold on, too, and yell to anyone who can hear, but my voice is nothing in the roar of a thousand wood years bending in a storm. A huge branch cracks above me and gets tossed like it's just a stick. *Where is the end of my rope?*

Hold on, knuckles white, limbs shake, won't stop. Shove tree dreams under my shirt to free my hands and try to pull myself up to grab the traverse, but somehow I release my rope instead. Falling now. *Oh my God.* Fly down forever until I remember *yank your rope.* I grab at anything until a yank jerks me stopped. *Idiot. Idiot. Idiot.* Everything tangled—my limbs, my ropes, trying to remember. *Why do I do these things?* If the wind would just stop, I could think straight and make decisions in all this rage. Chest rope. Harness. Foot knot. Stirrup. Haul my whole body. Chest rope. Harness. Foot knot. Stirrup. Haul my whole body up. Do it again and again until I reach the traverse line, grip the rope and pull, yank, and heave to wherever it goes.

Climbing gets harder, like I'm going uphill to where the rope is attached to a tree. Everything in me pulls the weight of me toward where the rope is tied. Titanic tree is not standing straight at all. Something else snaps off nearby and flies by my head. *This is it.* A dream catcher is tied into branches above where the rope is attached. I will have to climb. The first step is a nearby branch that I can almost reach. I let go of the traverse line, sit in my harness, and swing myself toward it. Miss it. Swing again. Miss it. Swing again, and this time I grab the branch under my armpit, hang on, and breathe before I haul myself up and sit. A wood island in the middle of no land. Branches like stairs lead to the dream catcher, which might be too far away from where my rope is attached to the traverse, but I don't care.

Gripping with my fingers I climb, digging into bark, trying not to slip on what is thrashing around, shivering and soaked, my rope stretching too far, pulling my harness down, until my butt barely makes it on to the top branch. It is so far to fall. Unhook the rope from my harness that attaches me to the traverse. I let it fly down and it dawns on me that I've done everything in the wrong order. I'm now unattached. Grab the dream catcher with one hand, the only thing connecting me to this tree, knuckles white from gripping so tight. The second rope is attached somewhere on my harness and I fumble to find where it is twisted around my leg. Once it is freed I wrap it around the branch, hook it into the net and slide onto the dream catcher. I take off my pack, shove it under my legs and lie back with my head near the trunk and my feet facing out to forever. Hold on and pray that I won't get ripped from the net that is bucking around. Whole body in a cramp, chilled in my bones. *Please make it stop*, I pray. I don't pray exactly except that I do, with every cell of me. Everywhere gray, wild, flailing branches, wind howling, and then a giant crack that sounds like a train crash that comes from I don't know where.

28

Thousands of bits of light look like they are falling from the sky. There are so many. Delicate seeds float down like snow. I want to catch them. I pull my sweatshirt away from me and hold it to make a bowl. I walk around in the falling, everything falling so gently. I want to catch all of the seeds of light. This worries me. Maybe I won't be able to. I start to run around the woods. They aren't falling fast enough. I never know where to stand. I watch one for a while, the way it drifts. It seems to take forever. I won't be able to catch it. That one is taking too long. I run somewhere else, to a light that seems closer, but that takes forever, too. I see another one, and if I just run fast enough I'll get to it. But, when I do, it lands on me and disappears like melting snow. I'll never be able to plant any of them if all they do is melt away.

Then the dream changes, as dreams do, and I am the one that's falling. I am falling so fast and hard I will break every bone. I know this. This is how I will go. I want to see Dad. Mom. Lily. I want to see Justin. I want to touch them one more time. Hug them all, tell them how much I love them, but I am falling too fast through branches. They whip me as I rush past. I fall hard onto them. It hurts my back. Everything falling. The forest. The sky. Everything I love. It's too late. I know this. Falling and feeling stupid, like such an idiot to think that I could catch a few silly little seeds, like planting them would stop all this. It's already too late.

And then, I am not falling at all. I am floating. I hear tap-tap-tap *just barely. Jade?* Tap-tap-tap. *I feel it on my chest. Over and over.* Tap-tap-tap, tap-tap-tap. *These taps on my heart, where the seeds are landing, sinking deep inside, reminding me that there is*

*nothing to catch. There is no falling. There is only knowing that the
light has already taken hold.*

Inside of falling it is quiet, even in the rage. I hold on to my net
so I don't fly off, but I let go, too. The seed in my heart starts it.
What is light. What knows. What is connected to everything
and forever. It spreads through me in an instant, and my body
lets go of its cramp, like I'm warm from the inside out. Keep my
eyes closed and go soft in my body, because the shiver and the
chatter and the panic and the clench will not get me through
this storm. I have never been here before, still in the middle of
magnificent, terrifying, deafening, super-powered swirl. I am
the anchor in me for however long it takes.

Forest thrashing gets quieter somehow, at some point, until
it's only a little wind and *tap-tap-tap* tries to nudge me awake. I
feel it before I see it. How I had been wrong all along. What the
tree in my dream was trying to help me see. That what is in the
tree is in me, and what is in me is in the tree, and how the name
of the light is no name at all. There is nothing to name, only
something to *be.*

Tap-tap-tap falls on my jacket, over my chest like a steady
drip. *Tap-tap-tap.* Water from some branch overhead. I open
my eyes, and I am still here, in this net, in this tree. Whatever
branch snapped off flew somewhere else. It's over. My dream.
The storm. Everything is soft-focus blurry—needle-green into
in-between gray into long fields of brown. Sunshine from somewhere dazzles in drops of water heavy like dew, the washed world
aglow.

AFTERWORD

**On how *Tree Dreams* jumped from the page
and into the world**

Highway 26 runs like a vein between Portland, Oregon, and the coastal town of Seaside, seventy-nine miles due west. Once you escape city limits, the road dwindles to two lanes that first cut across rolling hills of farmland and then head through the middle of forest thick with Douglas fir. You, in your little car, can feel like an intruder crawling over the feet of the forest that tower on either side of the road. It's dark and quiet and feels like you are driving through the middle of a secret.

This stretch of road is where I let my worried and jagged thoughts escape out the window. I didn't do this on purpose necessarily, but there is something about those trees that made me trade in my busy brain—the way they stood together, the gentle tangle of light and dark, the way the air smelled sweeter there, how they bent with the wind, the feeling of peace that hovered.

It used to be that you'd see clear-cuts in the distance—areas that are heavily logged in tidy, geometric shapes. If you've never seen a forest with clear-cuts, imagine your own head. Then imagine taking a comb and parting your hair into perfect squares and using scissors to cut your hair down to the scalp. Make other squares nearby, and keep snipping until your hair is long in spots and chopped in others and resembles a patchwork quilt. The overall effect would be odd and unsettling. And so it is in the forest.

For most of the decade that I lived in Oregon, the clear-cuts still felt far-off, something that happens somewhere else for reasons that don't seem to matter because they are far away. But one Sunday, on a drive to the beach, I was in road-trip position with my head lolled back against the headrest, arms hanging limp at my sides, and my eyes in a dreamy scan of the forest when a clear-cut popped into view just feet from the road. Behind a thin, peek-a-boo curtain of a few trees left standing, the stubble of hacked tree trunks and leftover branches marred the ground.

The forest is not mine, and I know this, but this clear-cut felt brazen, like the sudden appearance of a burglar in my bedroom. It crept up on me, and I couldn't figure out how it had gotten so close without my noticing. This is when my then-four-year-old daughter piped up from the backseat. "Why do the hills look so sick?" she asked. And it's true. They did look sick. I heard myself tell her something about needing trees for houses and floors and furniture, which is also true. But this was no answer. It was information. It did nothing to explain why the hills looked sick or appease the queasy feeling that precious secrets were being stolen from right under my nose or quell the sense that I was somehow just letting it happen.

It was around this time that I had a dream. In the dream I am standing in a forest under an inky dark sky. An oak tree looms before me with thick, snaking branches that kink and bend and reach and grow right before my eyes. Light glows from the tiny tips of each branch, the whole tree a giant glow-ball in the darkness. I bask in the luminous glow. There is something I need to do or know. I have had this dream before. It is my job, I think, to name the light. I don't know how I know that

I am meant to name the light or what will happen when I do. Wheels will be set in motion, perhaps. Or something important will shift. The problem is that for the life of me I can't remember the name. The light knows I know its name, as does the entire forest. Everything waits for me as I stand before the tree and search my memory.

The name is on the tip of my tongue. I feel it coming. I'm about to speak it when I hear a voice. "Mama, Mama." This throws me. I'm distracted. I hear it again, "MAMA!" I bolt upright, and my daughter is calling from her room across the hall. I stumble out of bed in a fog of waking worry for what's got her yelling. My feet shuffle themselves to her door as the rest of me tries to stay deep within my dream, desperate to remember and then speak the name of the light, wondering what epic event will happen when I do.

My daughter is cozy under her covers. "Mama," she says. "My feet are cold."

It's like she's speaking in a foreign language. "Your feet are cold?"

"Can you get me some socks?"

"Socks." I repeat. Socks and the name of the light.

I fumble in the dark for something to warm her toes. The cosmic timing is a joke, but I shove the wondering about the "why" of it from my mind and fight to keep hold of the thin thread of dream that just might connect me to the name of light. I feel around in the dark for socks and then her bed and then her little kid feet. I slide the socks on, kiss the warm soft of her forehead, and make my way back to bed. By the time my head hits the pillow, the dream is gone.

The feeling from my dream, however, stays with me. It creeps into daylight hours. I begin to notice every tree in my neighborhood, the lucky leftovers spared from urban development or planted afterward. They stand crammed into small lots and parking strips. Their presence is palpable—not just a green backdrop to the swirl of city life rushing around me, but living, breathing beings that inhabit the same neighborhood I do. I half expect them to start talking to me or throwing apples at anyone who treats them with disrespect, like the trees in the *Wizard of Oz*.

Would trees actually throw things?

My dream and the clear-cut forest along Highway 26 stayed with me like an imprint on a photographic negative. Their absence had a presence, and it haunted me. I had to do something. Doing nothing would be like seeing someone crying and not asking if he or she was okay. But, what to do? I decided to learn everything I could about trees with the hope that—well, I didn't know exactly. Maybe I could learn what would be helpful.

I discovered all kinds of amazing facts about the ways trees are connected with each other and the world around them in ways we can't see. For example, Professor Suzanne Simard of the Department of Forestry at the University of British Columbia discovered that trees communicate with each other through their root systems. If a tree has a disease it sends chemical signals to other trees alerting them to the threat. These trees then adjust their chemistry to protect themselves. I also learned how redwood trees are astoundingly resilient. My favorite fact is that when a redwood tree dies, its own roots give birth to new trees in a circle around where it once stood. These circles of new growth are called Family Circles, and you can see them all over redwood forests. While it is most certainly a survival mechanism, that particular form of survival struck me as quite dear, a way of coming together in loss, a kind of embrace.

Another fact was striking: one-tenth of 1 percent of all the seeds that fall from a Douglas fir actually take hold. The rest are blown away, are eaten by birds, are waterlogged, or succumb to some other bigger force. While a fact like that could make you feel cynical, somehow it gave me an incredible sense of hope. All those seeds that a tree generates feel like so many possibilities, so many chances to *be*. And when I looked around and saw how many trees actually do make it, all it takes for trees to live and survive, and then, even more, what they do for us—make the oxygen that we breathe, for one—it seems impossible that I never worry if there is enough oxygen. And yet, there it is. I breathe. And I write.

My research inspired another tree dream. Seeds of light fall from a tree, and I frantically run around trying to catch them. I plan to plant them. I have a hat in my hands, and I run from one falling seed to another, but my timing is off. The seeds fall at a mind-bogglingly slow rate, and I can't gauge my pace. What's worse is that they disappear like melting snowflakes just before they land in my hat. This worries me. I will never catch enough. And then, suddenly, I am the one that is falling from somewhere high up, crashing through branches at terrifying speed. I am sure I will die. I feel ridiculous for trying to catch seeds, for thinking I could plant them, that it would make a difference. It's too late. Too many trees are gone. *We are all falling* is what I think in the dream. And then, like dreams do, it changes again. I am no longer falling, but I feel a tap on my chest, over my heart, *tap, tap, tap*. A tingly feeling fills my whole body, and it dawns on me: there is nothing to catch. There is no falling. There is only knowing what is already inside. The seed is *in me*. I lie awake in the early morning hours feeling this tiny bit of knowing brighten me from the inside out.

At the time, I was in the midst of writing this novel. Jade took walks in old-growth groves or leaned back against the trunks of trees and absorbed gems of wisdom, as if the trees shared information with her, as they do with each other through their root systems underground. The wisdom was like a gift generously offered. She wrote what she learned on small tags and then tied the tags to trees so that others would happen upon them, read them, and come to know the voice of trees, too.

I became secretly jealous of her tree-tagging adventures. I wanted to tag trees. So I got in touch with a dear friend of mine in Portland who runs a small print shop called Cumbersome Multiples out of a garage in her backyard. She helped me create a kit that included small rectangles of recycled chipboard, twine, and a tiny book with a collection of tree facts and wise sayings about interconnection. We called our project Tree Dreams.

On my first tag I wrote, *Trees use sunshine to make the air that you breathe. What secret magic do you make and then give away?* On the next tag, inspired by the ways that trees give and take from everything around them, and concerned about our propensity to think of trees as an endless resource, I wrote, *Nothing works if there is only taking.* And then I went tagging.

Maybe, I thought, *this will connect me to the glowing tree of my dream. Maybe I'll remember the name of the light. Maybe I will finally speak the name aloud. What will happen when I do?*

At first I felt like a crazy lady tying messages to tree branches. Self-consciousness made my skin prickle. I also worried that I would get caught, though caught doing what I wasn't entirely sure. I wasn't committing a crime that I was aware of. We'd taken care to use material that would dissolve safely back into the earth. So I took the twine between my fingers, said hello to the tree that I was asking for the favor of adorning with a tag, and tied the tag loosely around a thin branch where it dangled in the breeze.

My friend and I created more Tree Dreams kits and asked others if they would tag trees, too. To our surprise, many said yes. Pretty soon Tree Dreams tags were hanging in countries around the world and across the United States, and teachers even began to make Tree Dreams curriculums.

Then came the tornado.

On May 31, 2013, four hours before the widest tornado in recorded history tore through central Oklahoma, my cousin-in-law, Tracie Alexis Seimon, tied a tag to a tree that stood outside of Sid's Diner in El Reno, Oklahoma. On the tag she wrote:

> *What we are doing to the forests of the world is but a mirror reflection of what we are doing to ourselves and one another.*
> ~ *Chris Maser*

Chances are very high that no one ever had the opportunity to read it.

Tracie is a molecular scientist for her day job. She was in the Midwest on vacation with her husband, Anton, a veteran tornado researcher and storm chaser who has conducted research for organizations like National Geographic. Chasing storms is an extracurricular activity for the Seimons, and they use vacation time to immerse themselves in massive weather systems. They have done this for years. On their trip that May, they also volunteered to be Tree Dreams taggers.

Their relatively routine storm-chasing trip took a tragic turn, however. Three of the Seimons' friends and colleagues lost their lives in the tornado that claimed five other lives as well.

But when Tracie hung her tag on the tree at Sid's Diner in El Reno, there was no way to know just how violent the storm would become. At that point, she simply wondered whether the tag would still be hanging the next day. She didn't have to drive very far outside of town before she knew that the chances were slim.

The tornado that swept through Oklahoma on May 31 grew in size from half a mile to 2.6 miles wide in a matter of minutes. It was so huge that, from up close, you couldn't see the sides of it—the swirling mass, with three-hundred-mile-an-hour winds, was simply all that you saw. It became a maximum-strength tornado, with wind speeds reaching EF-5 intensity, the highest rating possible.

Tracie's recollection of what happened next took time to piece together, but it included being caught in hurtling curtains of rain, trying to keep track of the multiple vortices that spontaneously emerged, and dodging flying debris. At one point, the tornado suddenly changed direction and increased in size and intensity to a degree that no one had anticipated. Luckily, the Seimons managed to break free from the storm's circulation and flooding rains and drove to safety at her brother's house—a drive that normally takes forty-five minutes but that took five hours due to the storm.

They spent the next thirty-six hours reconstructing the day's events—their route, the storm, and their relation to its movements—to better understand what had happened. They rested. They camped. They repeatedly Googled the names of colleagues who had not checked in to their usual networks.

It was Anton who finally saw the report at five in the morning two days after the storm: their friends and colleagues, storm researcher Tim Samaras, his son Paul, and their research partner Carl Young, had lost their lives to the twister. Camping out in a remote area in Colorado, the Seimons were in shock, trying to make sense of the whole experience. The storm was unprecedented, and in the many years that Anton has been a researcher and chaser, no one had lost their life.

Before leaving the Comanche National Grasslands in Colorado to drive to Denver for their friends' memorial service, Tracie tagged a cactus. On the tag she wrote:

> *Whilst this planet has gone cycling on according to the fixed laws of gravity, from so simple a beginning endless forms most beautiful and most wonderful have been, and are being, evolved.*
>
> ~ *Charles Darwin*

Apparently, the parking lot at the memorial service looked like a storm-chaser convention, packed with trucks and vans with weather-research whirligigs and scientific doodads. The service was packed. In honor of Tim Samaras, whose inspiration for storm chasing had originally come from *The Wizard of Oz*, they played "Over the Rainbow."

On the drive home to the East Coast, the Seimons passed

through El Reno one last time. Their first stop was Sid's Diner. Tracie's tag had been snatched by the storm, though the twine was still intact. They retraced their route, now marked by rows of leveled houses, trees stripped of their leaves, and branches and debris strewn in every direction.

Tracie decided to hang one more tag near the place where their friends had lost their lives. They pulled over at a wide, open field. Three trees remained standing. Only one, a Juniper, looked like it would actually survive. Wildflowers had bloomed at the base of the tree since the storm passed through just a few days prior. Tracie wrote:

> *If happy little bluebirds fly beyond the rainbow, why oh why can't I?*
>
> *~ Judy Garland*

In memory of Tim and Paul Samaras and Carl Young

When Tracie and Anton tied the tag, the two broke down in tears.

Tracie messaged me sporadically as these events unfolded, each message filled with still more unbelievable news. I read each text feeling increasingly helpless, not knowing what to say. In the face of such extreme weather, enormous loss, and the overwhelming fact of how small we are, words can feel insignificant—like the rectangular tag that was sucked up into the storm.

"And yet," I messaged her back, hoping to offer some bit of solace, "ideas and small acts can still buoy us, like a raft. They can never stand up to the terrible size of a tragedy like the tornado in Oklahoma, but they are like the few trees that are still standing in El Reno. They say, 'I am still here. I matter.'"

I was driving when Tracie replied, and I pulled over to read her message. I sat, breathless, parked on the side of the road, reading on the tiny screen of my phone.

"This project that you inspired us to participate in morphed unexpectedly into something of much deeper meaning during the course of our trip," she wrote. "It became so much more than spreading ideas about people's interconnectedness with nature and relaying a conservation message: we found we were creating a personal connection between the tornado (nature's awesome power), a surviving tree (nature's resilience), our friends (living out their dream), and us.

When we first learned that our friends were killed, I really regretted that we were on the same storm that killed them. However, after going back to the spot and tagging that lonely tree, this completely changed, and I actually felt relieved that we were there because it helped me understand what happened and better cope with the loss of our friends. It's like you wrote to me—it was a small act that buoyed us."

As I read her story alone in my car, a luminous thread shot back through moments in time—her trip through Oklahoma and all that transpired was somehow connected to the highway between Portland and Seaside, Oregon, to the secrets of that forest that drew me in, to my dreams of glowing trees and falling light-filled seeds, to how ridiculous it sometimes seemed to collect arboreal facts and write them on scraps of cardboard. Like the messages that pass through root systems for the benefit of the grove, an alchemical mystery ran through it all—a powerful concoction of words and wonder, love and good intentions, and generous acts that managed to transcend what seemingly separates us. For it is deep within the roots and trunk where the light abides, the power that connects us all.

ACKNOWLEDGMENTS

An entire ecosystem helped to bring *Tree Dreams* into the world. My arboreal education primarily took place in Oregon and Northern California, where many people were generous with their time, stories, knowledge and perspective—Peter and Pam Hayes, the thoughtful, enterprising and big-hearted duo behind Hyla Woods and the Build Local Alliance, shared their inspired vision for the future of our forests, and their Timber property as a site for a forest-based dinner series called Duff Dinners; Brooke Van Roekel created sumptuous feasts for Duff; Sarah Deumling graciously offered her insights and co-hosted a Duff Dinner at her family forest, Zena Forest, with the help of her daughter Katherine Deumling, who cooked up a storm; Sean O'Conner, Brian French, Will Koomjian and the rest of the crew at Ascending the Giants let me tag along as they climbed and measured the biggest tree of each species for the National Big Tree Registry; Portland Parks & Recreation's Department of Urban Forestry training allowed me to become a Neighborhood Tree Steward; many Oregon foresters, loggers and state and federal employees fielded my questions and offered their perspective; and a small group of devoted forest defenders told their tales of perseverance and bravery, taught me how to climb big trees and allowed me join their tree sit, the only one in the country at the time.

The Portland literary community is a treasure with many gems—The Pinewood Table offered support through many drafts under the wise and masterful guidance of Joanna Rose and

Stevan Allred; Jessica Morrell's keen eye steered the manuscript to steady ground; Mathew Stadler and Patricia No's Publication Studio supported the early work and participated in Duff Dinners. There were those outside of Portland as well. Immense gratitude to Ron Buehl who was one of the first to believe in Mazzy/ Jade and helped to shape early drafts. Scott Wolven and Shanna McNair of The Writer's Hotel were instrumental in the polishing stage. And Jamie Lunder, whose friendship, shared love of trees and the written word, and Lunder Award for Literary Excellence helped make everything possible.

The Tree Dreams tagging campaign leapt from the pages of the novel long before it was completed and in turn informed how the final pages were written. Tracy Schlapp of Cumbersome Multiples fortuitously gifted me flowers on May Day and helped not only dream up the Tree Dreams tagging kits but, with her antique letterpress and design brilliance, made that dream come to life. Yoko Ono said, "A dream you dream alone is only a dream. A dream you dream together is reality." Hundreds of Tree Dreams taggers have spread seeds of interconnection across the globe and endlessly inspire me with their devotion and love of trees and the natural world. Two Tree Dreamers, Tracie and Anton Seimon, tagged during the biggest tornado in recorded history and shared their incredible story with me, a story that has become Tree Dreams lore.

Many dear friends have read countless drafts and encouraged me to keep going: the one and only Sibyl Chavis, Justine Prestwich, Charlotte Fryer, Amy Critchett, Marie Sayles, Amy Novesky, Maura Conlon-McIvor, Tom Snyder, Zarka Popovic, John Calvelli, Gabriela Ammann, Glenn Motowidlak, who hiked with me in silence, and Tressa Yonekawa Bundren, who suggested I have one last go.

Finally, none of this would have been possible without my

own precious Family Circle—my parents, David and Allyne Kell-Pittle, and my sister, Karin Pittle-Gale, who have cheered me on every step of the way; my darling Siddha Rose, whose kid-earnest question about the health of the forest helped to set the Tree Dreams wheels in motion, and whose wise heart gives me hope for the future; and my husband Jeremy, whose eyes have been a refuge, and unwavering belief and support have always created solid ground, even when there was none.

ABOUT THE AUTHOR

Kristin Kaye is an author, ghostwriter and teacher whose work sits at the intersection of nature, narrative and spirituality. *Tree Dreams: A Novel* has given rise to a global tree tagging campaign that celebrates the myriad ways we are connected to each other, to nature and to our future. Tags hang in twelve countries and across the U.S. and *Tree Dreams* has been adapted for the classroom. Kristin's previous work includes *Iron Maidens: The Celebration of the Most Awesome Female Muscle in the World*, which details her experience directing twenty-five of the world's strongest and most muscular women in an off-Broadway show. The book was a finalist for the Oregon Book Awards, and described by *Utne Reader* as "one of 5 new titles for women who resist easy definition."

SELECTED TITLES FROM SPARKPRESS

SparkPress is an independent boutique publisher delivering high-quality, entertaining, and engaging content that enhances readers' lives, with a special focus on female-driven work. Visit us at **www.gosparkpress.com**

Ocean's Fire, Stacey Tucker, $16.95, 978-1-943006-28-1. Once the Greeks forced their male gods upon the world, the belief in the power of women was severed. For centuries it has been thought that the wisdom of the high priestesses perished at the hand of the patriarchs—but now the ancient Book of Sophia has surfaced. Its pages contain the truths hidden by history, and the sacred knowledge for the coming age. And it is looking for Skylar Southmartin.

Hindsight, Mindy Tarquini, $16.95, 978-1943006014. A thirty-three-year-old Chaucer professor who remembers all her past lives is desperate to change her future—because if she doesn't, she will never live the life of her dreams.

The *Alienation of Courtney Hoffman*, Brady Stefani. $17, 978-1-940716-34-3. When fifteen-year-old Courtney Hoffman starts getting visits from aliens at night, she's sure she's going crazy—but when she meets a mysterious older girl who has alien stories of her own, she embarks on a journey that takes her into her own family's deepest, darkest secrets.

Running for Water and Sky, Sandra Kring. $17, 978-1-940716-93-0. When 17-year-old Bless Adler visits a local psychic, the woman describes a vision of Bless's boyfriend, Liam, lying in a pool of blood—sending Bless on a 14-block sprint to reach Liam before she loses the only person she's ever opened her heart to.

Within Reach, Jessica Stevens. $17, 978-1-940716-69-5. When 17-year-old Xander Hemlock dies, he finds himself trapped in a realm of darkness with thirty days to convince his girlfriend, Lila, that he's not completely dead—even as Lila struggles with a host of issues of her own.

ABOUT SPARKPRESS

SparkPress is an independent, hybrid imprint focused on merging the best of the traditional publishing model with new and innovative strategies. We deliver high-quality, entertaining, and engaging content that enhances readers' lives. We are proud to bring to market a list of *New York Times* best-selling, award-winning, and debut authors who represent a wide array of genres, as well as our established, industry-wide reputation for creative, results-driven success in working with authors. Spark-Press, a BookSparks imprint, is a division of SparkPoint Studio LLC.

Learn more at GoSparkPress.com